D1611912

A KUDZU CHRISTMAS

A Kudzu Christmas

twelve mysterious tales

RIVER CITY PUBLISHING
MONTGOMERY, ALABAMA

Published in the United States by River City Publishing
1719 Mulberry St.
Montgomery, AL 36106.

Designed by Lissa Monroe

First Edition—2005
Printed in the United States of America
1 3 5 7 9 10 8 6 4 2

Library of Congress Cataloging-in-Publication Data

A kudzu Christmas : twelve mysterious tales / edited by Jim Gilbert and Gail Waller.— 1st ed.
        p. cm.
    Summary:"A collection of Christmas mystery short stories contributed by twelve contemporary Southern writers. Includes biographical sketches of authors"—Provided by publisher.
    ISBN 1-57966-064-9
    1. Detective and mystery stories, American—Southern States. 2. Christmas stories, American—Southern States. 3. Christmas—Southern States—Fiction. 4. Southern States—Fiction. I. Gilbert, Jim, 1966- II. Waller, Gail.
    PS648.D4K83 2005
    813'.087208334—dc22
                                        2005011991

TABLE OF CONTENTS

INTRODUCTION

Julia Spencer-Fleming

W hat do you think of when you picture a Southern Christmas? Frost riming the long needles of lollobby pine? Cornbread and chestnut stuffing in the turkey? The choir singing carols at the First Baptist Church?

Uncle Ray face down on the kitchen floor with great-grandmother's carving knife in his back?

My friends up in New England, where I now live, are never quite sure if they can believe my accounts of life as an expatriate Alabamian. Sitting in the parlor while a stream of elderly relations—all of whom are dressed better for "calling" than I normally am for churchgoing—discuss how much my children resemble people who were called to Jesus in the Eisenhower administration. Trips to Montgomery that begin with, "Since you're driving that way, you might as well stop by Montevallo and visit your cousin Marianne. You know she'd love to see you." (Marianne is my second cousin once removed, and the last time we had a conversation I was in preschool.) After-church family suppers in a restaurant owned by Cousin Callie and Cousin Sonny, where I discover that the amusing woman sitting across from me at the long, long table is my cousin Melva's husband's sister's mother-in-law's daughter. You know—family.

So you've got to know, if there's one thing Christmas in the South is about, it's family. And family can lead a sane person to want to murder.

Not, I hasten to add, any members of my own family, all of whom are sweet, agreeable, and good-looking. But I can imagine the impulse, and so can several of the authors in this collection.

In Patricia Sprinkle's "Angels Unaware," family duty means hauling everyone— and the turkey—down to the old Florida homestead to see what eccentric Uncle Jobo is hiding in the upstairs bedrooms. A home with a different and troubling legacy brings an estranged family together in Montgomery in Mary Stanton's "The

Groaning Board." Les Standiford reminds us that, like my cousin's husband's sister's mother-in-law's daughter, one of the "Wonders of the World" is that it doesn't take sharing genes, or even the same country, to make friends into family.

Dean James taps into a nearly universal fantasy (no, not the one about being a gay Mississippian vampire) when The Obnoxious Relative gets her just desserts in "It Came Upon a Midnight Dead." And just desserts—as seen through the fierce and unsentimental eyes of children—are also served up in "The Year Bobby Do-Wop Whacked Santa," by Shelley Fraser Mickle.

Surrogate families can turn toxic, too, as an English teacher beset by a campaign of lies discovers in Sarah Shankman's "Secret Santa." And in Michelle Richmond's "P.S. You're Mine" another young woman learns that family-destroying falsehoods come from without and within.

Mary Anna Evans takes us back to a Christmastime when "A Singularly Unsuitable Word" in the mouth of a child was enough to prove a man's guilt—and an innocence we've all lost in the intervening years. It's an actual child who is lost—left in the living nativity—in Carolyn Haines's madcap "Miracle Bones."

The holidays are often when we feel the absence of a loved one most. In Alix Strauss's "Swimming Without Annette," a bereaved lover deals with her loss by hunting down a killer—and finding a different kind of salvation in a Christmas memento. And for some children, salvation from the absence of love and care lies in imagination and wishes—but as Suzanne Hudson reminds us, occasionally, the answer to a wish is "Yes, Ginny."

Finally, in the moving "Welcome to Monroe," Daniel Wallace cuts to the heart of the mystery: Why? Why hate? Why love? And shows us the truth for one bereaved family: "People liked to read mysteries . . . but they didn't like to have them in their lives."

Twelve tales. Twelve views of Christmas, bleak and silly, cynical and magical, just like the real thing. Enjoy them with your own family this year.

And have a merry Christmas!

JULIA SPENCER-FLEMING is the Agatha, Anthony, Dilys, Barry, and Macavity Award-winning author of *To Darkness and to Death*, *Out of the Deep I Cry*, *A Fountain Filled with Blood*, and *In the Bleak Midwinter*.

ANGELS UNAWARE

Patricia Sprinkle

Usually we had Christmas at my folks' house and the whole family would come, but the year I was nine, Uncle Jobo called on Christmas Eve. Said, "I'm feelin' too poorly to travel." Said, "Think I'll stick around home this year."

And Mama said, "He hasn't wanted me down there since his last cook quit, over a week ago. Hasn't even fussed at me to find somebody to replace her. Something's going on, and I aim to find out what it is. We'll take Christmas dinner to Twin Planks. I'm going to have Phoebe cook a goose."

"Be careful, Caroline," Daddy warned. "The goose you cook may be your own."

Mama huffed her patented little huff of disgust. "We've got to do something. Jobo's too far from everybody out there."

Jobo lived at Twin Planks, the old Nadd place, where he had been born. A low white house with a tin roof and deep verandas on every side, it sprawled by the banks of the St. Johns River, surrounded by moss-hung live oaks that probably watched the first Spaniards float by. The St. Johns, a mile-wide sheet of black, cypress-stained water, flows steadily north until it bends east at Jacksonville on its way to the Atlantic. We lived on the river in Jacksonville, and I liked knowing that every drop of water had passed Uncle Jobo's on its way to us.

Members of the Nadd family had lived at Twin Planks since 1850 and made a good living trading up and down the river. The early ones traded cotton and lumber, and Mama bragged that Nadd boats slipped through Yankee blockades to supply the Confederacy with food during the war. Daddy bragged that Nadd boats supplied North Florida with most of its liquor during Prohibition. (Mama was scandalized whenever Daddy told that, but Daddy would just laugh and say it showed the Nadds kept their priorities straight.)

"I still want to go and see that he's all right," Mama insisted. "I worry about him. If he fell, he could lie and rot before anybody found him."

"Jobo wears that thingamajiggy around his neck. He can push the button and get help."

"If he remembers to push it. You know good and well his memory is shot. Half the time he calls me Maddie."

Maddie—born Madelaine Angela Nadd—was Mama's mama. She died before I was born, and I am Madelaine Nadd DuBose, after her, just like my brother, Barton, is William Barton Nadd DuBose II, after Mama's Granddaddy Will. It would have seemed fairer to me if one of us had been named after somebody from Daddy's family, but Daddy said having both Mama's children surnamed DuBose was about as much as he figured the Nadds could tolerate.

Uncle Jobo—Johnson Boswell Nadd—was actually Mama's great-uncle, the brother of her Granddaddy Will. At ninety-two, Jobo's heart was still pumping strong, but his mind was one egg short of a dozen. Daddy said God broke the mold when he made Jobo. Uncle Claude, Mama's brother, said God had nothing whatsoever to do with the creation of that cantankerous old coot.

But I liked Uncle Jobo. He pretty much let Barton and me do whatever we liked when we were down at his place, which was more than you could say for the other grownups in the family, so I defended him. "He doesn't live alone. He's got Clementine and Bray and Lulu."

Clementine was an elderly cow Uncle Jobo had raised from a calf. He claimed they were in a contest to see who could outlive the other. Bray was a broken-down donkey Uncle Jobo had rescued from a petting zoo after Bray started nipping at children. Uncle Jobo said that showed good sense, and he could use a little good sense around his place. Lulu was a sheep Uncle Jobo had won as a lamb in a poker game. The man who lost the lamb had offered to slaughter it for him, but Uncle Jobo said he'd wait 'til he had a taste for mutton. He was still waiting, and Lulu was almost as old as me. She followed him around the yard like a faithful dog.

"And Father Orville," added Barton with a snicker.

Mama didn't like Father Orville, an elderly Episcopal priest who lived in a fancy retirement center down river from Uncle Jobo. "He's not a good influence on Jobo," she told Daddy, "picking him up for that poker game every Friday."

"He also takes him grocery shopping and out to Sadie Lou's," Daddy pointed out.

"Yeah, but one of these days Jobo is going to lose both the house and the land in a poker game. You need to do something."

"It is Jobo's house and land, honey bun, and I'll try to keep a leaky roof over your head and day-old bread on your table for the rest of your life." To hear him talk, you'd never know Daddy sold more real estate than anybody else in North Florida.

Father Orville also picked Uncle Jobo up on Sundays and took him to church, but Mama didn't approve of the church, either. They sang happy choruses instead of slow hymns, and sometimes people spoke in what they called angelic tongues. Afterwards, Uncle Jobo and Father Orville ate at Sadie Lou's Kitchen, a little place down by the river, because Father Orville said his retirement home was run by Yankees who fed him nothing but undercooked vegetables and pap. I had no idea what pap was, but that's what he told me they ate.

None of us knew what Uncle Jobo was eating now that his cook had quit. She'd called Mama five days before Christmas to report, "I find it too much trouble to get myself way out there in the country every day to do for a man who complains about whatever I set before him. Besides, that is too much house for one woman to clean."

It was a lot of house. As generations of Nadds had borne more children and developed numerous hobbies—growing orchids, inventing gadgets, writing macabre stories, collecting antiques and paintings—they had built on rooms until the old place flowed in all directions. It had never had a real name, though, until the summer I was four and Barton eight, when a distant relative had fallen through one of the wide rotten steps leading up to the front veranda. Rather than fix the steps, Uncle Jobo just propped two wide planks across what remained of them and made a ramp. That was how you still reached the veranda. Barton started calling the place Twin Planks, and the name stuck. Even Mama called it that by now.

So on Christmas Eve, when Barton reminded Mama of Father Orville, she decided, "We ought to go on out to Twin Planks right this minute and camp out." (By which she meant we'd sleep in Uncle Jobo's dusty, chilly guestrooms.) "Cooking Christmas dinner in that impossible kitchen will be hard, but not as hard as toting everything and trying to keep it warm on the way."

I stamped my foot. "I'm not going out there on Christmas Eve. Santa won't know where to find me." I had written a long letter to Santa over Thanksgiving, asking for a bike and a dollhouse and a complete set of Nancy Drews, and I'd left the letter lying around so the family could read it before I mailed it. I already knew all there was to know about Santa Claus—including the fact that my parents were flat-out liars—and I figured this was the last year I could get away with pretending. I planned to make the most of it. (Barton had read the letter and said, with a sneer he practiced in mirrors, "Don't push your luck, kid." I stuck out my tongue at him, thinking Mama hadn't been looking, but she was, so I got punished. Barton never got punished for anything in his life except for saying there was a dead man under one of Uncle Jobo's beds—but that came later.)

Daddy backed me up about driving to Twin Planks that day. "You know we always go to the midnight service at St. Mark's, and Barton's supposed to read one of the scriptures."

"I don't want to," Barton grumbled. "Nobody's gonna be listening. They've all heard that story five million times." His voice dropped to a snarl, "'And an angel of the Lord appeared unto them.' Oh, puh-leeze. Have you ever seen an angel? Has anybody? Of course not." He clumped upstairs.

"Barton!" Scandalized, Mama started after him.

Daddy held her back. "Let him be. He'll read fine when the time comes."

Mama huffed a bit more but agreed to go to Twin Planks in the morning instead, then headed to the kitchen to help our maid, Phoebe, make pecan pies. After a while, Daddy called after her, "Did you let Jobo and Claude know we're all going down there tomorrow?"

"I called Claude. He has to pick up his kids, so he'll bring Daddy."

"Is he bringing his latest bimbo, too?" Daddy asked—but too soft for Mama to hear. Then he raised his voice again. "But have you called Jobo?"

She stuck her head out the kitchen door. "No. I want to find out what he's up to, so I don't want to put him on his guard. Lainey, I haven't heard you practicing piano today."

As I headed for the living room, Daddy muttered, "Lord, have mercy on us all."

Christmas day was gorgeous—warm, moist, and soft, with just enough motion in the air to set the moss swinging in the trees. Puffy white clouds hung over the river, and gulls swooped and swirled above the black water. I took deep breaths of air so sweet it could be served up for dessert and felt downright sorry for Yankee kids who had to bundle up to go outside, even if they did get a white Christmas. I didn't even need a sweater to ride my new bike up and down our drive. I had serious thinking to do. Santa had come through so magnificently, I was having second thoughts about his nonexistence. Mama would never have bought everything I asked for.

While I rode my bike, Barton tried out his new basketball—foolishly convinced that if he practiced enough, he could make the middle-school team—and Mama and Phoebe loaded up the car with goose, dressing, and all the other Christmas dinner stuff. Phoebe had done most of the cooking and Daddy had paid her extra to come with us to serve, but after they got the car loaded, Mama said, "I swear, I'm so tired after all that cooking, for two cents I'd send the rest of you down there to eat and I'd go back to bed."

We knew she didn't mean it. Mama never liked for Uncle Claude and his three kids to go down to Twin Planks if she wasn't going to be there.

She was afraid they would make off with some of the particular antiques she had her eye on.

In spite of the antiques, Twin Planks was practically falling down in places. I never knew if Uncle Jobo was poor, like he claimed, or lazy, like Mama and Uncle Claude claimed, or a man of other interests, as Daddy claimed, but his idea of home repair involved a lot of duct tape and baling wire. Still, the house looked pretty that morning, dappled with sunlight shining through the live oak leaves. We drove down the driveway to the patch of ground-up oyster shell in back where everybody always parked.

"Run in, Barton, and tell Jobo we've come to surprise him," Mama ordered. "We don't want to catch him in his underwear. Lainey, honey, carry these potatoes in to the kitchen."

Barton headed around front, his prized basketball under one arm. Mama handed me a cardboard box holding an enormous bowl of mashed potatoes surrounded by towels to keep them warm.

I had to walk carefully because the back porch steps weren't in much better shape than the front ones. After I'd managed to tug the saggy screen door open with both hands full, I let it slam behind me. As I crossed the worn linoleum to set the box on the scarred oak table, I heard a clatter. Out of the corner of one eye, I saw something white hurrying down the hall that led from the kitchen to what used to be the orchid greenhouse. Mama was going to have a fit if Jobo was letting Lulu run loose inside.

Right then, though, Mama was still loading Daddy and Phoebe down with boxes. On my way back to the car I dawdled to keep her from giving me a second turn, and looking up I saw something draw back from the window of the small second-story study added in 1890 by Swansea Nadd, who'd been a writer.

What was Uncle Jobo doing up there? His bedroom and the den were both off the front hall, so he rarely went upstairs. Besides, here he was now, coming onto the back porch in gray work pants and a plaid flannel shirt, his slippers slapping and his shirttail flying, screen door banging behind him. "You all put that stuff right back in your car and get on home, now. I told you, Maddie, I'm feeling poorly. Don't have the strength to entertain visitors." He waved both big hands. "Get on home, now." The wind ruffled the white hair circling his bald spot, and he squinted against the sun.

"I'm Caroline," Mama reminded him, stepping past him and onto the porch, carrying her green-bean casserole, "and the only thing wrong with you is, you haven't been eating properly. I've bought freezer containers, and I'm going to leave you enough prepared meals to eat for a—" She stopped on the porch and stared through the screen. "Who on earth cleaned up this kitchen?"

Now that I thought about it, I hadn't had any trouble finding a place to put the potatoes. Usually Uncle Jobo just shoved his last meal's dishes to the middle of the table to make space for the next plate.

"I know how to wash a dish." His voice was sharp. "Know how to cook, too, when I need to, so you come on back down off that porch and do what I say. Take that food home and eat it there. I got things I'm fixin' to do this afternoon."

"You're fixing to eat Christmas dinner with your family on Grandmama's Limoges," Mama told him. "Claude will be here in an hour with his kids and Daddy." Jobo started to protest, but she demanded, "You haven't lost those dishes in a poker game, have you?"

"I haven't lost a poker game in fifty years, girl."

The grownups kept wrangling, but I saw Barton motioning to me from a corner of the house, so I ran to see what he wanted.

"Something funny's going on," he told me in a hoarse whisper. "Uncle Jobo's room is real clean, and when I first went in he was sitting in his

recliner already dressed. There's a funny smell in his room, too. Come see!"
He was still carrying that basketball under one arm.

I followed him in. He hurried toward Uncle Jobo's bedroom, the third
door on the left of the large front hall. I paused to glance down the long hall
to my right, which led to the four guest bedrooms and the east side porch.
Was it my imagination, or had something white just crossed that hall?
Lulu?

I followed Barton to Uncle Jobo's room. "Smells like perfume," I
announced.

Barton let out of those nasty little snickers he'd been getting good at
lately. "You reckon the old booger's got a woman down here?"

I giggled. "I'll bet she's in one of the other bedrooms. I think I saw
somebody."

"Let's see! Be real quiet, now."

We tiptoed out and down the hall, close to the wall so the boards
wouldn't squeak. The guest bedrooms had last been decorated by
Granddaddy Will's second wife, Miss Lyddie, whom Mama described as "a
pastel women with unoriginal bad taste." She'd painted all the rooms white
and bought exactly the same curtains and bedspreads for each, but in
different colors—blue, pink, green, and lavender. Barton and I looked in
every room, in every closet, and in the two big bathrooms. We didn't find a
soul.

However, I did see droplets of water in one tub, like someone had just
drained it, and that made me think of something. I towed Barton by his
sleeve back down the hall and into the pink bedroom. "Why isn't this room
dusty? Even the mirror's been polished." I tiptoed over to one of the twin
beds and lifted the spread. "There's sheets and blankets on this bed!"
Normally the beds were bare, just covered for show. When visiting, we
always had to bring our own sheets.

"If somebody's in here," Barton said real loud, "you better come out quick, before my daddy and Uncle Claude find you. That's all I got to say." He stamped his feet like he was scaring rats, then kneeled down to peer beneath one bed ruffle.

I shivered. Suddenly I wanted to be with Mama and Daddy in the worst way. I dashed out of the room, down the hall, and into the kitchen, where the grownups' battle now raged—Uncle Jobo insisting he wanted no company for dinner and Mama insisting he was going to get it anyway. "You kids run outside and play while we get this meal on the table," she told me, not noticing I was alone.

I had just sulked out to the front-porch swing when Barton thundered into the front hall, yelling at the top of his lungs, "There's a dead man in the lavender bedroom!"

That brought Mama and me both running—her from the kitchen, me from the porch. "Who is it?" we asked at the same time.

Daddy passed Mama in a stride that let us know he'd already had enough of everybody for one day, even if it was Christmas. He grabbed Barton by one shoulder. "That is not funny, Bart. We've got enough to deal with, without silly stunts. Now get outside and play."

"But—"

"I said out!" Daddy smacked Barton once on the backside, jerked him by the back of his collar, and propelled him past me and through the front door. Cool, I thought.

Barton hit the ramp, tripped, and rolled to the ground, roaring in fury. "Okay, don't believe me. Go look for yourself!" He jumped to his feet and headed off toward the back of the house, so upset he forgot to take his ball. I knew where he was going—to the hayloft. That's where we always went when we got mad down at Twin Planks.

Daddy gave a huff that would have done Mama proud. "Let me go see what's got Barton so upset. Probably a rolled-up rug." He stomped down the hall.

Nobody noticed me, so I waited just inside the screened door. I heard Daddy make an odd, strangled noise, then he yelled, "Jobo, get in here!"

Uncle Jobo came out of the kitchen, hair standing on end like he'd been running his hands through it. Daddy met him in the front hall.

"What is it?" Uncle Jobo made it real clear he already had enough on his plate, dealing with Mama.

"There's a dead man under the bed in your lavender bedroom."

"I know that. If you all hadn't stuck your noses in—"

"Jobo, there is a man under your bed with a bullet hole in his head. What is going on?"

"I told you, I know that. It's nothin' for you to get all het up about."

"Jobo, did you shoot somebody?" Mama demanded.

"It's nothing to do with you."

"Nothing to do with us?" she yelled. "A murdered man in this house, me your only living relative, and it's nothing to do with us?"

"What about Claude? He's my living relative."

"Stop changing the subject. Did you kill a man? And stick him under your bed?"

"I told you, Maddie, it's nothing to do with you. Now, you all go on. Get out of my house so I can get the fellow in the ground before dark."

"Where in the ground?" Mama asked suspiciously.

"Up in the family plot. I already got the hole half dug."

"You can't dump a murdered man in our family cemetery!"

"Stop spluttering and go home, girl. I don't plan to dump him. Father Orville will be here any minute."

Mama's face turned as pink as Phoebe's cranberry relish. "Father Orville knows?"

"Of course he knows. I called and asked him to come over this afternoon to say a few words. Seems proper."

Daddy finally got a word in edgeways. "You can't just bury a murdered man, Jobo. The police have to know."

"Police don't have to know a damned-fool thing. Man's on my land, I'll put him in the family cemetery. Nobody has to know a thing."

"Why did you shoot him?" Mama was nearly screaming by now.

"Don't be silly," Daddy thundered. "Jobo didn't shoot him. He can't hit the side of a barn."

"Can, too!" Uncle Jobo waved one fist. "Shot at a buzzard and hit the barn. Musta aimed a mite low."

"So you did shoot this man?" Mama sounded like she was choking on her own spit.

Jobo flapped one hand in her direction and raised his voice to a roar. "Y'all go home!"

Out in the barn, Bray began, well, to bray. Clementine chimed in with a deep mooo. Lulu punctuated the chorus with an occasional baaa. And over it all rose a squalling cry, almost like a baby.

Mama pressed a hand to her heart, reeled through the double doors to the living room, and collapsed onto the sofa. "You've got a baby out here, on top of everything else?"

I decided to add my two cents' worth. "He's also got ghosts. I saw one in the study window, one in the back hall, and one down by the guest rooms."

Daddy took Jobo by one arm and propelled him to the nearest chair. "There's no babies, and there's no ghosts. Sounds to me like Bart chased one of those peacocks into the barn." Raising peacocks had been one of Jobo's more spectacular failures in the get-rich-quick department. All the birds had escaped his primitive chicken wire fence within a couple months, but a few still remained in the woods and occasionally turned up, scrounging in the garden and screeching to scare us all to death.

"It ain't no baby, and it ain't no peacock," Uncle Jobo muttered, sounding like he'd rather not tell us. "If you hafta know, it's my littlest angel."

At this, Phoebe, who'd been watching from the kitchen doorway, slipped away.

"Angel?" The way Mama said it, I realized she didn't believe in angels any more than Barton did.

That was such a shock, I almost missed hearing Uncle Jobo say, "Yup. Two big ones and one little one. Came down the river—" He stopped, getting that confused look he got so often in those days. "Oh, I don't remember when. Two, three days ago. Floated right up to my dock and flew off the boat."

Mama opened her mouth to speak, but Daddy motioned for her to hush. "They told you they were angels?" He sounded interested. Maybe he believed more than Mama did.

Uncle Jobo seemed to think so, because he answered like it was the first reasonable thing he'd heard all day. "They didn't tell me anything, because they can't. The two big ones speak in angelic tongues, and I don't have the gift of interpretation. But they are beautiful, with long flowing hair. When they hit land, they shoved the boat back into the river and ran straight towards the barn. But by the time I got there, they had disappeared. Musta flown away for a while."

Or climbed into the hayloft. Like I said, Uncle Jobo is one dime short of a dollar. But I loved him enough to want to help him out with this preposterous story. "And after a while they came back, right? So now they live in the barn with Bray, Clem, and Lulu?"

"Heck no, honey. I saw them peeking around the door of the barn later that afternoon and I invited them on into the kitchen. Had to use hand motions, of course. I don't speak Angel. They came in and ate some cold biscuits and fruit—all I had around here since that last girl you hired left me." He gave Mama a dark look like she had personally fired his cook. "Then I showed them the pink room, since it's got the twin beds, and motioned they could stay there if they liked. They all took a rest. The little one and his mama were so tuckered out, they slept all night and half of yesterday. T'other one, though, she's fixed me some right nice meals. Spicy enough for a man to taste what he was eatin'. And she turned the rooms out so, I hardly recognize the place."

"What do they have to do with the dead man in the lavender room?"

Daddy slid that question in so slick, Uncle Jobo answered without stopping to think.

"Not one blessed thing. I found him later, dead as roadkill, lyin' in my barnyard. I went out there to scare away a buzzard who was circling Clementine. She was lying down sunning herself, and the stupid-ass bird musta thought she finally died. So I grabbed my rifle, went out, and took a shot at the old cuss. Didn't hit him—" he slewed indignant blue eyes toward Daddy—"but I did hit the barn. Twice. Heard the bullets ping. And that upset Bray and Lulu, I can tell you that."

"And then you found the dead man?"

Uncle Jobo had to know Daddy was getting exasperated, but he refused to be hurried. "Nope, first I had to let Bray out for a little run, he was so upset about me shooting his barn. Had some trouble getting him to go back in, though. I'm not as spry as I used to be, and chasing a donkey takes it out of me." Uncle Jobo rubbed one hand over his bald dome like he was stimulating his brain. "I think it was maybe our third lap around the barnyard that Bray shied a bit, and I noticed something lying in the long grass, near the back fence. Turned out to be that man, with a hole in one eye. I figure somebody killed him and dumped him there, thinking this old place was deserted. But whoever he is, he deserves a Christian burial, so I drug him in and stowed him under the bed in the first room down the hall. I didn't want the angels stumbling over him unawares, and I didn't have time to bury him right then, what with needing to see what I could rustle up for their supper." He gave mother another dark look. "Yestiddy was Friday, of course, when we go grocery shopping and play poker, so—"

"And we can't let a little thing like murder interfere with poker," Mama muttered.

"Well, Jobo," Daddy said, "we do have to call the sheriff. Somebody may be looking for this fellow—maybe a grieving widow and children."

So Daddy made the call from the phone in the hall. It must have been a slow day at the station, because Daddy barely had time to find the bourbon and pour the adults a drink before a car pulled up. The deputy who responded had a very red face and trouble keeping his britches up, with everything he had hanging on them. He must of hitched them up five times, walking from the car to the front door. "You all got some trouble down here?"

"Just a little matter of an unexplained dead man." Daddy motioned for the deputy to follow, and I heard Daddy's voice, pitched real low, all the way to the lavender room.

When they came back a few minutes later, the deputy went to the phone in the hall and made a call. I heard him say, "Read me the description of that feller again." He listened, then asked, "And a mole beside his nose? Yep, he's down here at Mr. Nadd's place, shot clean through the eye. Send a crime team down here, and somebody to pick him up." He listened again for a moment, then hung up.

"Looks like you may be due a little reward," he told Uncle Jobo with a smile that split his face half in two. "Matter of a hundred thousand dollars. This feller has been bringing women into this country illegally and forcing them to—uh—"

His eyes met mine, and everybody remembered I was there.

"Lainey, honey," Mama said, "you run on outside and play. This is grownup business."

I knew better than to argue, but I went as slowly as I dared to the yard. Barton's basketball lay near the front steps, so I picked it up and started bouncing it against the twin planks. By timing the bounces just right, I could hear at least some of what the deputy said.

". . . migrant work sites . . . kept them in trailers . . . one girl he kidnapped . . . Venezuela, I think . . . daddy's a multi-millionaire . . . escaped last week . . . newborn baby . . . called her daddy . . . heading toward Jacksonville . . . hiding out . . . offered a humongous reward . . . dead or alive. But you'll need to . . . questions, Nadd . . . still murder."

That last word made me hold onto the ball. I heard Uncle Jobo protest, "I'm not answering any more questions. I already told you what I know. I didn't murder anybody, not even the buzzard I was aimin' at."

I crept up the planks and watched the deputy hitch up his britches again. "Maybe you aimed at a buzzard and hit the man. Maybe you hit him on purpose. But you got to come on down to the station and answer some questions."

I expected him to start saying what they always say on TV about "you have the right to remain silent," but Uncle Jobo wasn't silent at all. Neither was Mama, who was explaining to the deputy that she'd cooked a whole Christmas dinner and didn't intend to have Jobo miss it.

I caught Daddy's eye through the screen and started to bounce the ball again, but it got away from me and rolled all the way down the porch and off the far end. "Dammit!" I yelled. My parents reached that porch in less time than it takes to tell it, and four eyes looked down at me in a way that let me know I was in almost as much trouble as Uncle Jobo.

"You march right to the nearest bathroom and wash your mouth out with soap," Mama ordered. But Daddy put out a hand to stop her. He was making funny motions with the other hand, pointing to the porch floor, then at the house, then to the far end of the porch.

"Deputy, come here a minute."

The deputy lumbered out, swinging his cuffs.

"What if the bullet didn't go directly from Jobo's gun to the man? What if Jobo hit the barn, but the bullet ricocheted and hit somebody hiding down near the end of the barn?"

"And hit him square in the eye?"

"No way Jobo could shoot somebody in the eye. Heck, he can't normally hit a barn."

"There is that," the deputy agreed.

"I did hit the dadgum barn," Uncle Jobo yelled from the living room.

Daddy made the same motions with his hand—to the floor, the house, and the end of the porch. The deputy made them, too. Finally he nodded. "Could be. I'll ask the coroner to check the angle of entry and whether it could have happened like that. And detectives will be out to check the barn. I guess it could have happened. Mr. Nabb is damned lucky at cards. Maybe he's a damned lucky shot, too."

Nobody suggested he go wash his mouth out with soap.

The deputy thought for a moment, then said, "How about if I leave Jobo out here until we get a coroner's report and information from the barn? You don't think he'll try and leave the county, do you?"

"I'm not goin' anywhere," Uncle Jobo roared. "I've been sayin' all week I'm too poorly to travel. Too poorly to have all this commotion, too. Why doesn't everybody clear out and leave me be? Take your food, go home, and eat it." Nobody paid him one speck of attention.

The deputy started down the planks, then turned and called through the screened door, "Don't reckon you could tell me the whereabouts of two women and a baby, could you?"

"I can't tell you a blessed thing," Jobo hollered.

The deputy's cruiser had barely crunched down the drive and away before we heard that squalling cry again, clearly coming from the barn. And this time we could tell, it was no peacock. Mama, Daddy, and I skedaddled to the barn, leaving Jobo on the porch, rubbing his head.

Lit only by sunlight streaming through the hayloft trapdoor, Phoebe shared a bale of straw with another woman, who wore a long black braid down her back. Clementine chewed her cud to one side of them while Bray nibbled hay on the other. Lulu lay on a pile of straw in front of another bale, where a young mother with hair like a blue-black waterfall cradled a tiny baby in her arms. Barton stood behind her, peering down at the baby. From the look on his face, I had the feeling he now believed in angels.

From the look on Mama's, maybe she did, too.

But I was puzzled. Why would angels be wearing Miss Lyddie's old white dressing gowns?

Uncle Jobo came up behind us and whispered loudly to Daddy, "Didn't I tell you I had me three angels? Aren't they the prettiest things you ever did see?"

Daddy reached out and grabbed him around the neck in the crook of one elbow. "Not all angels are pretty, you old cuss. Seems like there was one around here last week ugly as a junkyard dog, but he saved three lives. Name of Jobo, I hear."

Uncle Jobo shook his head. "I didn't shoot anybody."

"Of course you didn't. You just got yourself a sure 'nough Christmas miracle. Caroline, didn't you say something about a goose? And aren't Claude and his crew due here any minute?"

"Not to mention Father Orville," I added.

That got Mama's attention. "Phoebe! We need to get dinner on the table. Looks like we'll have extras to feed, and one of them's a priest."

Phoebe rose with a look on her face like she was floating back down to earth. She plumb loved babies, angel or human. "They's plenty of food, Miss Caroline. You know we always fix enough to feed a traveling army." She turned and spoke words I didn't understand to the young woman beside her. The woman smiled and answered in words like soft running water. Phoebe brought her toward us. "Maria, here, says she'll be glad to help me serve the meal."

Uncle Jobo looked down at me, delight and astonishment in every wrinkle on his face.

"Don't that beat all? Trust Maddie to find herself a maid who speaks Angel."

Raised in North Carolina and north Florida and held fast by Southern roots wherever else she lived, PATRICIA SPRINKLE has authored two novels, *The Remember Box* and *Carley's Song*, and several nonfiction books, including *Women Who Do Too Much*. She was challenged by her husband, Bob, to write her first mystery "to pay for the ones you keep buying." Since her first was published in 1988 she has published fourteen mysteries in two series, with a third series about to begin. Married for more than thirty-five years, Sprinkle and her husband have two sons, Barnabas and David.

THE GROANING BOARD

Mary Stanton

I know better, I do. Even so, my imagination periodically takes flight as it did after Grandma called. Uncle Sterling had put his mother, my great-aunt Levis, in a nursing home. There was no remedy, Gram said, but to sell her big house in Montgomery and move up to Atlanta to be closer to poor Aunt Levis.

"But Grandpa built that house," I groaned, although that was the least of what troubled me. The happiest summers of my life had been spent on Felder Avenue, and I couldn't imagine anyone but Gram ever opening that front door. A wise woman would have made her peace with what appeared to be a reasonable, if unhappy, decision made by other family members. But no. The difference between me and the wise woman is that she wouldn't have promised to come home for Christmas.

"I think I can get a direct flight from LaGuardia if I book early, Gram," I said. She thought that was an excellent idea. An hour later, after the magnolias choking my better judgment wilted, I recalled exactly why fewer and fewer of us had been gathering at Gram's. In a weak moment I'd cast my lot with the hopeful and simply chucked all my hard-earned experience.

When I called next evening intending to explain how I couldn't believe that I'd forgotten I had brain surgery scheduled for December 25, Gram had already lined up Sterling and Levis, the Kincannon cousins, and my mother.

"Sterling and Levis sitting at the same table? I thought they weren't speaking," I said. "Wait. How is Levis getting to Montgomery?"

Maybe I hadn't understood completely, Gram said. It must have been the poor phone connection. Montgomery was experiencing an unusually rainy winter, and that tended to fritz the lines. See, the place in Atlanta wasn't exactly a nursing home. It was more like a retirement village, and Sterling was footing the bill. Gram wasn't exactly selling the big house either. After all, as I'd reminded her, the Dobbins homestead was the work of my grandfather's hands. She'd need to think more about things, maybe go up and stay with Levis awhile before making any big decisions . . .

"What about Mother?" I barked.

"I told you, your mother's coming," Gram laughed. What in the world was the matter with me? Seems like I'd lived among the Yankees a day too long. And, oh yes, I might bring a big bottle of that nice New York City red wine if it wasn't too much trouble.

GRAM AND HER SISTER, Aunt Levis, are what all the Dobbinses, with the exception of my mother, call "vague," the family euphemism for those of us who keep things back—generally, but not always, important things. Neither of them out and out lie, and it isn't mental defect or even orneriness, but it is downright annoying. They've lived together since 1978, when Levis's husband, Borden, drank himself to death, and sometimes they appear to speak a language only they understand. My mother, Louise Dobbins Hampton Chenault, periodically declares herself sick and tired of both of them.

"Mama's manipulative, and in that sugar-sweet way of hers she always gets what she wants," she says. Mother also accuses Gram of reorganizing the past to suit herself. "She lies and then Levis swears to it." I think that's a bit harsh considering most of the people I know do the same, more or less. Gram is just more brazen about it.

Gram adores Aunt Levis, who, unlike her, is tall and thin and very soft-spoken. She loved to tell me what a beautiful debutante Levis made in 1951 and how their parents sent her to Europe to complete her education. This inevitably drove my normally cool and cynical mother to sputter, "Nobody came out, and there was no grand tour!" Truth is that Levis had gotten involved with a wild young man whom my great-grandfather despised, and he must have been some piece of work considering Levis married Borden with her parents' blessing. Anyway, since the family didn't have any money to speak of, Levis was packed off on a steamer bound for London to live temporarily with distant relatives who agreed to treat her like their own and keep an eye on her for six months, which they did.

Gram's claim that she had convinced Mother to leave her gated Amelia Island hideaway and drive down to Montgomery for Christmas without her brand-new husband, Moneybags, stretched her credibility so thin that it snapped. I simply did not believe her. Gram was good, but even she wasn't that good. So, I called my mother.

"I'm worried about her," Mother said in a small voice I hadn't heard since I fell out of the tree behind the big house and she took me to the hospital to get my leg set.

"Why?" I asked.

"Did she tell you that she was setting a place for Grandpa?"

There it was.

DESPITE MY MOTHER'S EASY accommodation to Moneybags's lifestyle, she'd actually been a peace, love, and rock-and-roller in her prime. In 1968 she protested the Viet Nam war at the Democratic National Convention in Chicago. To her everlasting credit, now that she's able, Mother gives a lot of money away and isn't flashy about it either. Being rich doesn't always make you a bad person. She and my grandfather argued for years about the South, Viet Nam, and especially race, but it's Gram she's never forgiven. I know why, although I try periodically to forget about it. The apple doesn't fall far from the tree.

After Mother accepted that she'd made all the points she was ever going to make with my grandfather, they became sufficiently civil. Though neither one ever backed down, the family was, for a time, able to celebrate Christmas together. We'd drive down to Montgomery from Atlanta and stay a full week. As a child it was impossible for me to understand how Mother could have so many problems with this gentle and loving man who thought that I hung the moon. Despite their admirable self-control, once in a while the old conflicts surfaced, irritations escalated, and they'd loudly and angrily attempt to redeem themselves in the other's eyes. And then, in the spring of 1994 a sudden heart attack took him from us.

Gram was inconsolable. She and Grandpa had enjoyed each other for nearly fifty years with an enthusiasm I still envy. Mother and I had flown to Montgomery to help her sort out the paperwork that invariably follows the end of a long and productive life. We weren't there but two days when Mother found the membership card that very nearly destroyed what remained of the Dobbins family.

In 1955, Townes A. Dobbins, Jr. paid a $3.50 initiation fee to Montgomery's White Citizens' Council, which had been established that year to maintain segregation in the wake of the famous *Brown v. Board of Education* decision. Anyone, black or white, who supported school integration was targeted by these "councilors" and soon found themselves suffering rent increases, evictions, loss of credit, and even mortgage foreclosures. The idea was that economic hardship would drive integrationists North, where they belonged.

Mother demanded to know why she'd never been told. With all the shrillness of the betrayed she challenged my grandmother to explain the terrible family secret.

Grandpa had been an officer of the Guaranty Insurance and Loan Company for almost forty years. He made decisions about whose loan applications got accepted and whose mortgages got renewed. Mother was horrified. Her worst nightmare was coming true. She wanted to know what kind of people she'd come from and how she was ever supposed to hold her head up again.

"You don't understand," Gram explained. "In those days everybody signed just to prove we weren't in favor of the federal government taking over the schools. Lawyers and businessmen joined, teachers and nurses, preachers, even the mayor was a member. It wasn't the Klan, Louise."

"It *was* the Klan," my mother thundered. "The damn white-collar Klan."

Gram put on a sweater, left the house, and didn't return until Mother was safely back in Georgia.

That Christmas I was the only member of my immediate family invited to dinner. Daddy was living in California by then, and Mother was waiting for an explanation, an apology, or some meaningful breast-beating before she'd even consider setting foot on Felder Avenue.

The battle continued by phone all Christmas week. Above the din of the Mormon Tabernacle Choir I heard Gram growl, "He was thirty years old, Louise, and you were only four. Your grandparents and Levis and Borden were all living with us, and Levis was pregnant with Sterling. Borden couldn't find his behind in the dark. Who was supposed to pay the rent and buy the food? Townes had no choice."

I just knew my mother would drag out her all-purpose litany, "Everyone always has a choice," right then.

"That's all well and good, Louise, but you don't remember what it was like. Your father never went to any of those meetings. He was just trying to take care of us."

I don't know what Mother said to her, but Gram's face went crimson and she hung up without letting Mother finish. "Well, Levis," she sighed, "Louise believes we should have sold this mansion and used our millions to move up North."

"Last time I looked, Louise was still living in Georgia," Levis said. "I'm going to make tea. Anybody want a cup?"

LAST CHRISTMAS, ONE BY ONE, Gram shamed us all into coming home. The notion of selling the old house that I'd loved so much and avoided for so long got me packing. Mother's conscience responded on cue to a threat of impending senility, and the Kincannon cousins were reminded, however subtly, that they still owed Gram money. Only Levis and Sterling arrived with light hearts.

Mother went into a snit as soon as she realized she'd been had. On Christmas Eve she announced that she was suffering a migraine and went off to bed. After she left, Gram peered at me and asked over her reading glasses, "Are we to assume you'll soon be visited by the spirits of diarrhea, croup, and colic?"

"No, Gram. I'm perfectly fine," I sighed, ladling another cup of eggnog fortified with enough brandy to resurrect Uncle Borden.

"That's my girl." Her face softened. "This is going to be a very special Christmas."

"What are you up to?" I asked warily.

"Trying to set things right is all," she said. "It appears in some people's minds I'm long overdue."

"You just need to tell her that Grandpa was wrong," I said, nodding toward Mother's room. "That's what she wants to hear."

"How can I?" Gram asked, her face clouding. "If Townes didn't sign up we'd have starved. His job would have been gone in a minute. People who crossed those monsters didn't work, banks wouldn't take their business, and grocers wouldn't sell to them. He did what he had to."

"Did he foreclose anybody, Gram?" In my heart I knew he must have, especially since he kept his job.

"I don't know. I didn't ask and he didn't say."

"And why did he keep the card?" The brandy was softening my brain and loosening my tongue. "Why didn't he just throw it away?"

"Because it shamed him," she huffed. "Your Grandpa wanted to remember what he'd done. He never forgot what we almost became—what some of us did become. Louise can't understand that. She'll never accept it."

"Well you could try—"

"A hair shirt does not become me, sugar," she said, rising up to her full height in the old wingback chair.

"Don't we know it," Levis laughed.

"Levis," Gram gently scolded, "let me tell the story."

"Not much of a story, is it?" Levis asked, ignoring her. "We let the bullies run things back then. You can dress a pig in an evening gown, but she's still going to be a pig."

Gram shook her head, but Levis continued. "When we were little, honey, our mama used to say that everything was possible at Christmas. All the world's rules get suspended one day a year. Do you believe that?"

"Why not?" My head was spinning. What was she talking about? What did Christmas have to do with Grandpa? But even a wise woman would have had a hard time resisting the twinkle in my aunt's deep blue eyes.

GRAM SET OUT A traditional Christmas groaning board with all the trimmings: her roast turkey with cornbread dressing, Levis's baked ham with apricot glaze, oyster casserole, pearl onions, rutabagas, turnips, corn soufflé, candied yams, and hot biscuits. Pumpkin and mince pies, sugared pecans, and banana pudding sat waiting their turn on the sideboard.

She'd also set a place for my grandfather right at the head of the table, just as she said she would. Mother rolled her eyes and declared in a stage whisper, "She never gives up."

"An admirable quality," Gram assured her.

"I'm comforted, Charlotte," Mother sniffed, (she'd begun calling Gram that after Grandpa died.) "It saves me worrying that you might be losing your mind."

"My mind is fine, thank you, Louise," and she announced that she would say grace. When Gram nodded, Levis rose, retrieved a book from the breakfront and delivered it as if she were presenting the crown jewels to Queen Victoria.

"Townes just loved William Butler Yeats," Gram said, as if it were something we all knew. I'd never seen my grandfather open a book, let alone a volume of poetry, but maybe Aunt Levis was right—Christmas was a time of miracles.

Blissfully ignoring of the rest of us, who by that time were nearly addled by hunger as we stared at the feast, she cleared her throat and began:

"I am content to follow to its source

Every event in action or in thought;

Measure the lot; forgive myself the lot!

When such as I cast out remorse

So great a sweetness flows into the breast

We must laugh and we must sing,

We are blest by everything

Everything we look upon is blest.

Amen."

We looked across the table, from side to side and back and forth, searching each familiar face for some flicker of recognition or understanding. It wasn't to be found. Gram sighed, and looking very satisfied, began passing the oyster casserole and candied yams.

We ate, mainly in strained silence. Finally, the miracle arrived, apparently on schedule, along with dessert and to the accompaniment of "Come Thou Long Expected Jesus" on the old stereo. Gram had served up the banana pudding and Levis added cream and passed them around. When everyone had a dessert and the coffee had been poured, Gram sat back and cleared her throat once again.

"I'm so pleased that you all came home for Christmas," she began sweetly. Mother behaved admirably. She never flinched. "I can't believe it's our tenth Christmas without Townes, but his spirit fills this house. He's with us right now—I believe that."

Everyone smiled sadly.

Gram shook her head. "But this isn't a time for sadness, and I don't want to go off on any tangents today. To put it plainly, Townes has left a Christmas gift for me to deliver."

If a pin had dropped at that moment it would have sounded like the Westminster chimes.

"What might that be, Mama?" my mother snapped, no longer able to contain herself.

"Townes Dobbins has given this house to Alabama State University."

"What?" five of us shouted at the same time.

"You heard me."

"He told you that, did he, Aunt Charlotte?" Sterling asked carefully.

"'Certainly not! Your mama and I have been thinking about this for a long while, and we figure it's the best way to finally set things right."

"What things?" I asked, just to break the uncomfortable silence that followed Gram's comment. I knew only too well what things.

"Well, it's no secret to anybody that fifty years ago Townes paid an initiation fee to that White Citizens' Council, and he felt diminished by it for the rest of his natural life. He wanted to make restitution but could never figure how."

"He gave to the NAACP," my mother whispered, her eyes riveted on the banana pudding.

"Well, yes he did, Louise, but he always felt that they were such a big organization, you know, and the people he'd offended were right here in town. Most of them are dead now, and God called Townes before he could decide what to do."

"But you and Aunt Levis have decided?"

"Yes, Louise, we have. Alabama State can have this house and use the money from its sale to start a scholarship fund for Montgomery's black kids. It's a black school, you know, so they'll know best what to do."

"But the house, Aunt Charlotte?" my cousin Bootsie Kincannon wailed. "How could you give away your house?"

Gram stared at Boots as if it puzzled her how anyone could be so dense. "Because Townes built it, Boots-honey, built it with his own hands.

It's his gift. We made a mess of things, and it's all past fixing for the black folks who were injured. What we can do is make restitution to their grandchildren."

"But what about you?" Bootsie's sister Mildred asked.

"I've led a good life," she said defiantly, "and the house is dear to me only because of Townes. It's his legacy to the university—to Montgomery, really."

My mother's mouth was hanging open at a very unattractive angle.

"Look, Louise," Gram said. "I don't know anymore what was right. I've been so sure for so long that Townes had no choice, but maybe you have a point. Maybe he should have held out, and other people might have taken strength from him and held out too. I just don't know. Maybe if we'd gone to the poorhouse over the whole thing we'd be in better standing with God and each other. Anything is possible. But I can live with this, and I know that your daddy would have done it if he'd thought of it first."

"Oh, Aunt Charlotte, that's so beautiful," Bootsie gushed, and Cousin Mildred's head began bobbing up and down like one of those annoying little dolls that people used to put in the back windows of their cars.

Suddenly there wasn't a dry eye at the table. Mother was actually sobbing into her linen napkin. Gram reached over and patted her hand.

"It's a wonderful thing you're doing, Aunt Charlotte," Sterling said. She nodded and made a gesture worthy of the Royal Family.

"But where will you live?" the ever-practical Cousin Mildred wanted to know.

"Well, I'll spend summers in Atlanta with Levis."

"And the winters?" Mildred whispered.

"Right here, of course. There's no place like Montgomery in winter."

For the first time I considered that Gram just might be losing her mind.

"But Aunt Charlotte," Boots stammered, "if Alabama State owns the house—"

"Yes, honey, they do own it, but they'll have to wait until I'm dead."

Mother's head shot up. "Dead?"

"The lawyer called it a backwards mortgage—a back-end mortgage? Something like that," Levis said nervously. "Charlotte can use the house for the rest of her life."

With black mascara still running down her cheeks, my Mother began to laugh. Her high wild cackle caught on like lace curtains in flame, and before long we were all doubled over and slapping at the table.

"I'd like to know what's so funny," my grandmother huffed, but no one could catch a breath long enough to tell her—and who would have been able to explain it anyway?

GRAM AND AUNT LEVIS FINISHED the winter in Montgomery and went on to Atlanta in the spring. They got us all to promise to spend next Christmas on Felder Avenue. I expect most of us will make it, but a year is a long time and the Dobbins family pot is always in danger of being stirred. Despite her new role as a philanthropist of sorts, bygones are not completely bygones between my mother and Gram. We could all end up right back at square one.

Last time I called Mother she said that under all that feigned confusion Gram's got a mind like a steel trap. I might be mistaken, but I thought I heard admiration in her voice.

And why not? After all, Gram succeeded in making a down payment on Grandpa's debt at no cost to herself—she gets to live in the house he built for her as he wanted her to, and as far as leaving it to any of us, well, she's right: there's no one who needs it bad enough for her to have considered it. She reasons that Mother and Moneybags will shore me up should I fall on hard times; Sterling, who's got no wife and more money than God, will see to Aunt Levis; and she let Bootsie and Mildred off the hook for all their loans.

Gram is like those white ladies who drove their black maids and nannies back and forth to work during the Bus Boycott fifty years ago. They insisted they did it because they couldn't manage without household help—not because they believed that segregation was wrong; yet they helped to end it. It wasn't the kind of aid anyone would ever want to count on, but it was something. And Grandpa? Well, no matter how dearly we all loved him, well, I guess we'll never really know.

"What your grandpa did back then is between him and God," Gram says, "and God moves in mysterious ways." Well, so do she and Levis. In my experience they've always been as elusive as God and all His angels, maybe more so. Suffice it to say that we Dobbinses pay our debts. It may not be everything, but it's something, after all. At least I think it is.

MARY STANTON is the author of two prominent civil rights biographies, *From Selma to Sorrow: The Life and Death of Viola Liuzzo*, (University of Georgia Press, 1998) and *Freedom Walk: Mississippi or Bust*, (The University Press of Mississippi, 2004). Stanton has taught at the college level and was a member of the faculty of the Writing Program at Rutgers University. Her articles have appeared in *Government Executive, Southern Exposure*, and *The African-American Experience: Personal and Social Activism in the 19th and 20th Centuries*. She currently serves as deputy administrator for the town of Mamaroneck in Westchester County, New York.

Wonders of the World

Les Standiford

I t was in Turkey that things took a turn for the better. I had
lagged behind the rest of the tour group, who were scattering
over the treeless hillsides, snapping pictures of the ruins,
complaining of the 10 A.M. heat, already chattering about the
promised "swim-stop" on our way back to Kusadasi to reboard the
cruise liner.

We had just completed our guided tour of the ancient city of
Ephesus, had seen the site of the Temple of Artemis, one of the Seven
Wonders of the Ancient World, and now we were having "free time for
your photos and browsing in the gift shop."

I had enjoyed these excavations, which to my mind outdid the
Acropolis in certain ways, and my Instamatic had fallen into the bear
pit in Bern, so I was free of that obligation. Besides, I liked the look of
this gift shop. A ramshackle series of interconnected cinderblock huts
with woven roofs, it provided cool shelter from the blazing Levantine

sun, and, more important, reminded me of little shops I had frequented in the Caribbean islands, not far from my Miami home.

Unlike most of the gift shops we had been herded into from Avon to Zermatt, this one reeked of straightforward deceptiveness. There were no practiced entrepreneurs to lead us past artisans cutting mosaic stones or carving out cameos, no lectures in impeccable English describing the myths embroidered on Grecian urns thrown before our very eyes, no tours of fragrant woodworking rooms spiced with authentic recorded folk music of the Alps.

Here, only a horde of distinctly eager shopkeepers with keen eyes and dark hair, several for each nook in the dimly lit labyrinth, and the unlikely background syncopation of Aretha Franklin pumping steadily from a stereo hidden in a recess somewhere in the maze.

I wandered through the twists and turns of the shaded arcade, drawn toward the throb of the familiar music, casually surveying the stacks of hand-tied rugs and bright embroidered blouses, refusing the incessant offers of full-color photo collections of the ruins.

"Much better than your own pictures, sir," one vendor said, nodding with assurance.

"You're right about that," I told him, but kept my lire in my pocket.

For one thing, I preferred my mind's eye recording of the broad main concourse that curled past one impressive reconstruction after another. My vision of a gang of Hadrian's troops jostling one another up the steps of the city brothel on a port call Saturday night seemed eminently preferable to any suitable-for-framing shot of its dusty, bank-like portico.

For another, I was traveling on a budget. The trip arrangements alone had been expensive—more, it had struck me as I handed the travel agent my check, than my father had earned most of the years of my youth. One evening the year I turned nine—I remember because it was Christmas week—he had come home flushed, announcing an amazing stroke of good fortune: his raise to the astronomical rate of sixty dollars a week. My mother set to dancing with him, and I went into a swoon at the prospect of some fabulous Christmas present, maybe even a non-hand-me-down bicycle.

In any case, I was still a bit guilt-stricken at my outlay for the trip and had determined not to squander my bit of mad money. We had yet to visit Dubrovnik, Florence, and all of France—I felt certain there'd be plenty of souvenir shops still to come.

I rounded a corner, deep in the warren of shops now, and realized I had come to the source of the music. A moment before, one earthen wall away, Aretha's pleas for R-E-S-P-E-C-T had sounded mute, even plaintive. Suddenly, it was an overwhelming demand. In the dim light, someone darted across my path. There were muffled voices and the music snapped off. A curtain flew back, and the room blazed with light.

I blinked, my nose wrinkling at a pungent odor. By the time my eyes adjusted, I already knew I was inside a room full of leather goods, but what an array this was: there were racks and racks of overcoats jammed top to bottom on the walls, coats of brown, black, and suede, coats of ankle-, calf-, and knee-length; a hundred or more vests, some lined with sheepskin, others unlined; row upon row of purses, dangling so low from the ceiling I had to duck; and under the window, a long line of slacks and skirts in a wild array of colors that danced and trembled as I brushed by.

Three young Turks looked proudly at me from their various stations, arms folded before their chests. They were smiling at my amazement, and I worried immediately that they had mistaken it for eagerness. It was a remarkable display in an otherwise commonplace arcade, and I was sorry that I couldn't buy anything from them.

"I liked the music," I said, waving toward the boom box, which hung at a tilt from a peg in the plastered wall. "You don't have to turn it off."

The one in front of me, in his thirties perhaps, an Omar Sharif double, broke into a grin. "Hey. All right!" He spoke in imitation of American slang and nodded to his friend by the machine. "I have the Pointing Sisters, too." He made a gesture that approved my choice as Aretha returned, softer this time.

"This is fine," I said, still taken by his patois. "I like your shop."

He nodded, quickly back to business. "Then you want a coat, maybe?"

I smiled but shook my head.

"Well, then," he paused. "What else? We have it all, you see." He swept his hand expansively about the room. The others, who I guessed spoke no English, nodded agreeably as he continued. "Very good prices. Maybe a purse. For your wife?"

I shook my head again. "I'm afraid not." We had divorced nine months prior to this tour. In fact, I had given the trip to myself as an impulsive gesture. It seemed an appropriate way to spend my half of the proceeds the attorneys had left. I would see something of the world I felt I'd missed. We had been so young.

My host seemed disappointed but put his hand out for me. "I am Ben," he said. "And you are from the States?"

I nodded and spoke my name as I took his hand.

"I attended university in Philadelphia," he said. "And I learned your music there as well."

"It's good music," I said. We all smiled and nodded. There was a silence as the tape reversed. "I've missed it," I added.

"I know," he said, still nodding.

I looked at him. He knew? It must have been a Turkish commonplace.

"So, you like this Ephesus?" He gestured brightly outside, at the dusty expanse beyond the shops, at the shards of columns poking from a nearby hillside. He spoke the name of this place with such authority, I thought. The syllables rolled with possessive fondness off his tongue.

"Very much," I said. "I've seen the Acropolis. And Pompeii. And the palace of the Minoans on Crete." He nodded in turn, waiting for me to continue. "But here, well, I am able to imagine what it must have looked like back then. The ruins are so much more intact, I mean."

He was still nodding, his face growing serious, and I went on. "It's as if I can feel the way real life was here, the little houses, the baths, the brothels . . ."

His eyes lit up at that, and his broad smile returned. "Ah! So they show you the little sign to that place, too?" He made the universal coital gesture with his hands, and everyone laughed. Then he seemed to think of something.

"Hey!" he leaned toward me. "You want something to drink? It's hot, no?"

I checked my watch. There was plenty of time left, and I'd made it clear I wasn't buying anything. "Sure," I said. "Why not."

He spoke in his language to one of the others, who darted from the room and quickly returned with four tall Cokes. The shape of the bottles was familiar, but the white lettering was stenciled in Turkish script. I tried to pay, but Ben refused.

"To the States," he said, raising his bottle. "And good music."

"And to Turkey . . . and Ephesus," I said, attempting to mirror the quick roll of his speech. We all drank deeply. Even warm, the liquid felt marvelous in the dusty heat.

He put the Pointer Sisters tape on, then turned to me as a horn arpeggio blasted into the stillness. I glanced out the window, saw one of our group trying to steady himself on the hillside above, his camera aimed at the shattered columns. I wondered if he could hear the music.

Ben took my arm. "Listen, agabey," he said, glancing conspiratorially at me, then at the doorway where I'd entered. He pulled me away from the window. "I have something. Not expensive. Something special for you."

I also looked nervously at the doorway. Was he going to offer me hashish? A currency deal? A woman?

I felt a nudge of sadness at this turn of our traveler's friendship but reminded myself that business was business. I should have seen it coming. I would finish my Coke and beat it out of there as quickly as I could. They had warned us on the ship. The Turkish authorities were not to be taken lightly.

Ben, meanwhile, had dropped to his knees and was parting the ranks of the racked skirts beside us. He pushed them aside to reveal a heavy strongbox the size of a beer case snugged up against the plastered wall. He had the lid up quickly and pulled out a smallish pouch.

"Look," he said, motioning me nearer. I glanced again at the doorway, then stepped reluctantly his way. He worked at the drawstring of the pouch and shook something into his hand. He took my wrist in a firm grasp and pulled me close. This was the moment, I knew, when the Turkish police would burst into the room, guns at the ready.

I stared down. A cluster of vague, irregular shapes the size of shirt buttons lay on his upturned palm. He took my hand and let these nuggets tumble into my palm. He let me go, and I moved to the window.

In the light, the buttons were transformed. I saw that I was holding a dozen or more semiprecious stones into which signet designs had been carved.

"Coins," he said, quietly. "From the ruins." He gestured out the window. "It was the money for them."

I stared back, trying to keep the skepticism from my expression. It was another of the scams they'd warned us about on ship. The vendors might try to sell us "relics," ancient artifacts made up the night before and scorched with fire or blackened with acid. We weren't to fall for it.

"Is that right?" I said, examining the stones more carefully. One tiny design in coral had caught my eye. A man in a tunic was seated on a stone, playing a lyre, while a woman in a simple gown and diadem stood nearby with her hand lightly touching his shoulder.

"How about this one?" I asked, pointing.

"Ah," he smiled at me as if I'd found the choicest one. "Very pretty, agabey. Byzantine, not Roman. Very old. Fifth century." I knew he meant B.C.

Outside, our guide was bleating the little air horn she used to herd us about with, a sound that cut sharply through the music. I glanced at the stone again. The tiny spires of the woman's crown radiated delicately about her regal head. A star shone down upon the tableau, its slender beams of light stretching toward the ancient pair. All of it done in a space the size of my smallest fingernail. He would have been up all night, even if he had faked it.

"I search the grounds when the tourists are gone," he looked at me. "And the guards, too, of course. They don't permit it."

The air horn sounded again. "Agabey," I repeated. That word he'd been using. It rhymed with *bobby*. "What does that mean?"

He looked out the window, smiling. My traveling mate who'd been photographing the columns was picking his way awkwardly down the rocky hillside, sliding from bushy handhold to handhold in his slick oxfords.

"Precisely?" Ben shrugged. "Is big brother. But here in Turkey, means *friend*. That's how friends are here. Each to each. Big brother."

I stared at him, at his easy grin. I'd been in Mykonos two days before, had heard two men arguing violently outside a tavern where I sat passing the time of day with the bartender. The bartender had explained that I needn't worry, that the men were good friends. "It is nothing," the bartender assured me. "If Greeks really care, they play outrageous jokes upon one another: 'Ah, you like my dinner, Philipe? Too bad, I feed you the meat of a cat, ha ha.' That's how friends are here," he'd said.

Now I was in Turkey. Agabey. Big brother. My friend Ben. The signet felt like a piece of history in my hand. The couple looked as if they'd been together two thousand years, might manage two thousand more.

Ben turned to me, his eyes pinched in concern. I could see from this distance that his shirt collar was frayed. None from our group had found their way to his distant shop. "Well," I began, still wary.

He held up his hand to stop me. "For you, agabey . . ." He named a price that seemed absurd. Less than the lunch tab I'd run up at the Greek taverna. It seemed insufficient, even for a night's work at forgery. And for a relic, it was impossible.

We shook hands again, and I had to run to make the bus.

A WHILE AFTER I RETURNED from that trip, I sat down before my first Christmas tree in a long time. I handed over the small box, which I had wrapped in white tissue and blue ribbon. Outside, the wind was brisk and the sky suitably gray, the driven mist as close to snow as a winter in the tropics could ever provide.

Inside, I had a fire crackling in the rarely used fireplace, and I'd dug out some carols for the tape player. There was a tang of pine in the air, and the retriever kicked and snuffled in his sleep.

She glanced at me, then worked at the ribbon and opened the box.

"It's beautiful," she said, turning the stone so it caught the light. There was a simple gold mounting that held it now, something fashioned by a jeweler I'd found down in the Keys. I'd ambled into his shop, drawn by its Dickensian name.

"Just look at them," she was saying.

I nodded. The two-thousand-year couple circled by a person named Whitfield Jack in present-day gold. There seemed some continuity in all that.

"What do you call it?" she asked.

I thought for a moment. Her eyes were shining in the light from the fire. "An agabey," I told her. "It's Turkish. It's rare."

"Oh," she said, clasping the chain around her neck. "Well, I love it. I love you." She smiled, and leaned close.

I put my arm around her. It wasn't necessary to tell the whole story. She'd never been to Turkey. She took it for exactly what it was.

LES STANDIFORD has authored an extensive library of books including *Done Deal*, *Presidential Deal*, and *Bone Key*. He wrote the screenplay adaption of his 1991 novel, *Spill*, which aired on Showtime, and the nonfiction work *Last Train to Paradise: Henry Flagler and the Spectacular Rise and Fall of the Railroad that Crossed an Ocean*. He is a frequent reviewer for major newspapers including the *Chicago Tribune*. His accolades include the Frank O'Connor Award for Short Fiction, a Florida Individual Artist Fellowship in Fiction, and a National Endowment for the Arts Fellowship in Fiction. He lives in Miami with his wife and three children, where he is a professor of English and director of the creative writing program at Florida International University.

IT CAME UPON A MIDNIGHT DEAD
(A Simon Kirby-Jones Story)

Dean James

In the old days I would have been in a coffin, dead to the world in the cargo hold of the airplane, rather than in first class.

I much prefer first class.

I glanced at my traveling companion, Giles Blitherington, sound asleep beside me. Since becoming an official couple, we hadn't spent much time apart. Upon deciding I could no longer put off a visit to my family in Mississippi, Giles had insisted he come with me.

"But what about spending Christmas with your mother and sister?" I had asked, half-protestingly. "Surely you wouldn't want to be away from them at such a time."

"Mummy's headed off to Italy with a group of Old Girls from her school, and Alsatia," his nostrils flaring on the name, "is skiing in Switzerland with the groom or garage mechanic of the moment."

"Well, then, I suppose I'll just have to take you with me to Mississippi."

Giles had grinned, and my heart, were it still able to beat, would have thumped loudly in response. He is very attractive, and when he hadn't tucked tail and run after I confessed to him several months ago that I am a vampire, he only endeared himself to me further.

"I think it should be great fun to meet your family. They cannot be any more annoying or eccentric than mine."

I had foreborn to comment. Time enough for explanations later, perhaps while we were driving from the airport in Jackson to north Mississippi, where my remaining family lived.

Giles stirred, blinked awake, then focused his eyes on me. He stretched, shifted his seat into the upright position, and suppressed a yawn. "How much longer?"

"Not much longer, love," I said. "The pilot announced we're making our descent into Jackson about two minutes ago."

"I'll be quite glad to get off this plane," Giles said. "I've never been in the air this long before."

"We still have a bit of a drive once we're on the ground," I said. "After we retrieve our baggage and get the rental car, it's about ninety minutes to my cousin's house."

"And on the way, you're going to confess everything about your barmy family?" Giles grinned at me again.

I laughed. "Yes, some of it, but you'll enjoy finding out some things for yourself."

Nearly half an hour later, bags stowed in the trunk of a rented Mercedes, we were on our way out of Jackson and headed north. Giles glanced at his watch. "Three P.M. I believe I'm jet-lagging. Surely your cousins will have some food for us when we get there."

"Oh, no worries about that. You'll get plenty of good Southern home cooking."

"Hog jowls and collard greens?" Giles laughed.

"Not quite. My family is a bit more sophisticated than that." I tried frowning at him, but he only laughed harder.

Giles gazed out the windows as we drove. He had never been in the United States before, so everything was new and interesting to him.

"Mississippi is a beautiful state," I said. "Still lots of undeveloped areas. There'll be gentle hills and plenty of trees where we're going."

"Lovely," Giles said. "Now, stop stalling, and start dishing on your family."

I sighed, pretending reluctance. "Very well." There was one bit of information that I was truly a bit reluctant to share, but there was no help for it. "The first thing is that the family name is Jones. Just plain Jones, not hyphenated Kirby-Jones. And they call me Sam, the name I was born with."

"Sam Jones, eh?" Giles chortled. "The dashing vampire Simon Kirby-Jones is really Sam Jones? This is too, too delicious, Simon. Should I start calling you Sam, too?"

I glared at him. "Don't you dare. My full name is Samuel Kirby Jones. Kirby was my mother's maiden name. I was never too fond of 'Sam,' so I rechristened myself 'Simon' when I was fifteen. My parents, God rest their souls, didn't put up any fuss, but the rest of the family can't remember."

"Very well," Giles responded. "I shan't call you Sam."

"Now that that's settled," I said, "I'll give you the brief version of the family tree. My grandmother, Nanny Mae Jones, is ninety-seven. Until a couple of years ago she was still very active, but she's becoming increasingly frail. Mentally, she's just as sharp as ever. She's the main reason I decided to come to Mississippi for Christmas. She never batted an eye when I came out to her, and she has always encouraged me to follow my dreams. I owe her a lot."

"Then I can't wait to meet this extraordinary lady," Giles said.

"She is that. The other members of the family you'll meet are mostly cousins. Granny lives with my cousin Clement and his wife, Lurlene. Clem's father was the oldest son, and my father was his younger brother. Then there's Clem's sister, Addy, who's married to Hobart Binks." I had to laugh, thinking of the brood of Binks offspring. Giles was in for some amusing times.

"What is it?" Giles asked. "What's so funny?"

"You'll find out," I said. "Addy and Hobart have six children. Three pairs of twins, actually. Rather a handful while they were growing up. I guess the oldest two are in their late twenties by now, and the youngest two just started in college."

"All of us are staying in this one house?"

"Yes," I said. "The house was built by my great-great-grandfather Jones in the 1880s. It's been added to several times. There's something like twelve bedrooms and nine or ten bathrooms. So there's plenty of room." I laughed. "You didn't think we would have to sleep on the floor on pallets, did you?"

"I was beginning to wonder," Giles admitted. "Is that all the family?"

"Clem and Lurlene have three children, but they won't show up."

"Why not?"

"You'll see soon enough. Let's just say Lurlene is not a happy woman, and she takes great pains to share that unhappiness with anyone who comes within a half-mile of her."

For the rest of the drive we chatted about sights along the way. The sun shone brightly on this December 23rd, with Giles seeing Mississippi at her winter best. I felt pangs of nostalgia the closer we came to my grandmother's house, out in the country several miles from Grenada, the nearest town.

When we arrived, I parked our rental car behind the dusty Ford pickup belonging to Clem. Giles stood beside the car, gazing at the rambling, two-story clapboard house. The sun was beginning to set, casting a rosy glow over the house and the ancient oak and elm trees around the yard. The lawn was a bit bedraggled, the flowerbeds overrun with dying or dead weeds. The house could use a new coat of paint as well, I thought.

The screen door banged open, and Clem stepped out onto the porch. "Simon! It's good to see you."

I stepped forward to take Clem's outstretched hand as he clattered down the steps from the porch, touched that he had called me Simon. "Clem, it's great to see you, too." It was, but I was shocked by his haggard features. He was nearly two decades older than I but looked even older.

Clem pumped my hand, repeating how good it was to see me. With my free hand, I gestured for Giles to join us. Clem finally let go, and I turned to grasp Giles by the arm.

"Clem, this is Giles Blitherington, my partner. Giles, my cousin Clement Jones."

Clem cut me a sideways glance before sticking out a hand to Giles. I had told him I was bringing my partner with me and had just assumed Clem would understand I meant another man. But apparently he hadn't. Clem had always been very sweet, if not exactly the brightest bulb in the packet. Which was the only explanation for his marriage to Lurlene.

Giles thanked Clem for his hospitality, and I could see Clem struggling with Giles's aristocratic accent.

"We're both delighted to be here," I said. "It's great to see the old home place, Clem." I moved toward the porch steps, the two of them trailing in my wake. "How is Granny?" I asked as I opened the front door, motioning for Clem and Giles to precede me.

"Pretty fair," Clem said. "She has her days when she don't get up to much. But knowing you was coming home for Christmas has perked her up real good."

Just then, the shrill tones of Lurlene's voice cut through to us from deep inside the house. "Clem! Where the hell've you got to? You know it's time for my medicine! I'm gonna have one of my spells!"

Clem scurried off, saying over his shoulder, "Be right back with y'all in a minute."

Giles arched an eyebrow at me, and I shrugged. "He can't get more than a few steps away from her, poor sod." Then I grinned. "You'll have a new appreciation for your mother by the time we get back."

He rolled his eyes. I stepped across the hall toward the room into which Clem had disappeared. Might as well get it over with.

We entered the front parlor of the house, which now looked more like a hospital room. Lurlene lay on a sofa, wrapped in quilts. Clem was handing her a glass of water and a pill. Lurlene popped the pill into her mouth, downed the water, and thrust the glass back at Clem. "Don't put me through that again, Clem. You know my heart can't stand the strain. Where were you?"

"Lurlene, honey," Clem said, his voice placating, "I told you a car drove up. Lookie here, honey, here's Sam—I mean Simon—all the way from England to see us. And this here's his friend, Giles."

I stepped forward, but Giles stood as if frozen to the spot. With my hand behind my back, I gestured for him to join me. He shook his head as if to clear it, then stepped next to me.

I looked down at Lurlene. She was a sight to behold. She had on enough makeup for the entire student body of a clown college, and her hair was so shellacked with spray, it wouldn't have moved in a tornado. Despite her ailments, which were as legion as they were imaginary, she maintained an enthusiastic appetite, as evidenced by the ample girth swathed by two of my grandmother's best antique quilts.

"Hello, Lurlene," I said. "No need to ask how you're doing. Still got that nasty case of *malingeritis eterna*, I see."

She had all the intelligence of a retarded lab rat, so the insult went right over her head. "Hello, Sam. I can't believe you had the gall to bring your boyfriend with you. Your poor mama and daddy are spinning in their graves because of you." She smiled, with malice. "And I can't help it if I'm sick. It's all them pesticides my daddy used when I was growing up. No telling what all I breathed in when I was a girl."

"How awful for you," Giles said.

"Yes, isn't it?" I said. "And isn't it amazing that with all her trials and tribulations, dear cousin Lurlene maintains such a sunny disposition?"

Giles started coughing, and Clem turned his head. Lurlene stared up at me in outrage. Even she wasn't stupid enough to miss the insult this time.

Before she could say anything, I spoke again. "Clem, is Granny in her room?"

"She's out on the sun porch," Clem said, bravely ignoring his wife and her mumbled rumblings. "We turned it into a bedroom for her this summer, 'cause she don't get up and down the stairs so good anymore. I know she's anxious to see you both."

"Thanks. Come on, Giles." I bowed to Lurlene. "As usual, dear Lurlene, it's been completely distasteful." I turned and marched away.

Giles laughed, following me down the hall toward the back of the house. "I see you weren't exaggerating. She is truly awful. Even Mummy seems a model of compassion and intelligence compared to her."

"Yes, well, she's made Clem's life hell for over thirty years. I don't know how the poor devil has stood it this long, but he's never had the gumption to divorce her or push her in front of an eighteen-wheeler, which he should have done long ago. There's absolutely nothing wrong with her except utter selfishness and bone-deep laziness."

I knocked on the door that led onto the sun porch. "Granny, it's Simon. Are you awake?"

"Come on in here, honey. I can't wait to see your sweet face."

Relieved at the strength of her voice, I pushed open the door. She sat near the windows that ran the length of the porch, wrapped in quilts, her head tilted to one side.

Her eyes still burned brightly in her ancient little face, but her hair was sparse now, and her skin mottled with age, as I could see from the one hand holding the quilt close to her body. I faltered for a moment at the shock of seeing her so old and so close to death. I should have come home to see her before now.

Dropping to my knees in front of her, I laid my head in her lap, as I had often done in childhood. Her small hand stroked my hair. I wanted to cry, though that was no longer physically possible for me.

"Honey, it's so good to see you," she said. "Now stand up and let me get a look at you."

I complied, and she smiled. "Handsome as ever. You look wonderful. Now introduce me to this young man of yours."

Giles had again hung back near the door, and I reached out toward him. He came forward to stand beside me, grasping my hand. "How do you do, Mrs. Jones? I can't tell you what a pleasure it is to meet Simon's grandmother."

She held out her hand to him, and he took it. She smiled up at him. "I'm glad to meet you, too, son. I can see now why Sam—I mean Simon—has been so happy. You're very good to him, I know. Now, y'all pull up a chair and tell me all about living in England. I always wanted to go there and see everything, but I never did."

We found chairs and drew them up next to hers. I talked about Snupperton Mumsley, the Bedfordshire village where we resided, and Giles added amusing anecdotes about people in the village. We chatted for nearly half an hour, until I saw Granny had dropped off to sleep in the middle of a story about Lady Prunella and the butcher. Giles and I stole away to let her rest.

Dinner that night was a painful affair. Clem, who always did most of the cooking, had worked hard, and the food was excellent. Lurlene, however, was at her poisonous worst. She found fault with everything and had Clem hopping up and down to fetch things for her. He ate very little himself, and I could see why. Lurlene was enough to kill anyone's appetite.

When Clem brought in dessert, Lurlene and I spoke at the same time.

"Lemon icebox pie," I said, "my favorite!"

"I can't believe you made lemon icebox pie," Lurlene moaned. "You know how it upsets my stomach."

"Then perhaps you shouldn't have any," Giles observed.

Lurlene's face reddened. "Who the hell are you to talk to me like that?"

Granny, who had been quiet during the meal, dropped her napkin on the table. "Lurlene," she said, "We've all had about enough of you. I am ashamed to have guests in my home who have to listen to you and your never-ending whining. So shut up!"

I stared at my grandmother. I had never heard her use such a tone with anyone, not even Lurlene.

Granny smiled across the table at Giles. "I'm tired, and I'm going to rest. Would you mind helping me to my room?"

"I'd be delighted, Mrs. Jones," Giles said, rising from his seat.

Lurlene, her face now bright red, had been shocked into uncharacteristic silence. I helped myself to a slice of lemon icebox pie while Clem stared at his wife.

Once Giles had escorted Granny from the dining room, Lurlene pushed herself back from the table and clomped out, still not saying a word.

I turned to Clem. "That was an excellent dinner." I doubt he had even noticed that the portions I had consumed were very small. "Why don't you go and relax now. Giles and I will clear everything away."

"Thanks, Simon. I could use a breather." His face was gray with exhaustion. "Just leave Lurlene's things to me, though. I'll take care of them later."

"Certainly," I said. I had noticed that Lurlene's plate and drinking cup were different from everyone else's.

"She can't bear to use things that anyone else has used, so she has her own special stuff," Clem explained. "She likes for me to make sure it's all properly cleaned."

Just another way for Lurlene to control him, the poor sod.

As if my thought had cued her, Lurlene bellowed from across the hall, "Clem! Where are you?"

Clem tensed, and a telling expression crossed his face but was quickly gone. I could see that on some level he hated her but didn't have the nerve to do anything about it. Maybe I'd offer to pay for a lawyer for him so he could divorce the witch. But on some other level, did he even want to be rid of her?

Clem left to answer his summons, and I started clearing the table. Giles returned a few minutes later to help, saying that Granny was sound asleep. We made short work of the task, and when I suggested we retire early to our room, Giles didn't argue.

"I don't want to spend any more time tonight in the vicinity of that harpy," he said as we climbed the stairs to the second floor.

"She's even worse now than she was before," I said, opening the door to our room. Clem had prepared for us the same room I had always had as a child whenever visiting my grandparents, and I appreciated him for remembering.

Exhausted from the long flight and now full from dinner, Giles was ready for sleep. I needed very little rest, but I didn't mind lying in bed with Giles sleeping next to me. He always slept very soundly, and if I slipped away during the night to write, he never seemed to mind. I wouldn't do that while we were here, but I could at least lie in bed and work on the plot for my next book.

Giles woke about seven the next morning. I loved watching him wake up. He smiled at me and yawned. Then he pulled me to him for a morning kiss.

Sometime later, showered, dressed, and ready to face the day, we went downstairs. We found Granny in the kitchen, sitting in her motorized wheelchair and busily working on something at the table.

"Good morning, Granny." I leaned down to kiss her cheek. "What are you making?"

"Good morning, honey," she said. "Morning, Giles. I hope y'all slept well. I'm making eggnog, of course. You know it wouldn't be Christmas Eve without eggnog."

"It sure wouldn't." I winked at Giles. "Granny's eggnog is something everyone should taste at least once." It was potent, to say the least. A few sips, and Giles would probably be flat on his back.

Giles helped himself to the scrambled eggs, bacon, and biscuits Clem had left on the stove for us. I nibbled at a biscuit for form's sake. All I really needed in the morning was the helpful little pill that made my existence as a vampire in the twenty-first century a blood-free one.

"What are Clem and Lurlene up to this morning?" I asked.

"Same as always. She's running him ragged, pretending she's dying," Granny said, her voice tart. "She can't stand the fact that he paid any attention to anyone but her last night, and she's making him pay for it today."

"Why hasn't he divorced her?" I asked. "If it's a matter of money, I'll be happy to give him whatever he needs."

Granny smiled and reached over to pat my hand. "You're sweet, honey, and Clem ought to take you up on that. But that fool boy feels like he owes her. He married her, and he's going to stick by her. For better or worse. He really believes that." She shook her head. "But she's sucking the life out of him, drop by drop, and he can't see it."

Giles and I exchanged glances. I wasn't the only vampire in the family after all. But Lurlene was worse, feeding on the life and emotions of other people. "I wish there were something I could do," I said.

"Don't you fret about it," Granny said. "The Lord will provide, somehow." She regarded me with those bright eyes. "Now, there's something I want to tell you. I may not be around much longer, and I'm trying to get everything settled before I go."

I started to protest, but she held up a hand. "No use talking about it. The Lord has seen fit to give me ninety-seven years, and I'm not asking for more. I'm tired, honey, and I'm ready to go, so don't you be fretting for me."

"Yes, ma'am," I said over the lump in my throat.

"There's a box upstairs in your room," Granny went on, "and I want you to take it back to England. There are some special things in it, things I want you to have. Everything else I'm leaving to Clem and Addy. Clem will have the house because he's done his best to take care of it the last ten years. You're doing real well, aren't you? You don't really need any money?"

"No," I said. "Clem and Addy should have whatever you want to leave them." What Granny had given me over the years was far more important than money or property, and she knew that.

"I knew I could count on you," Granny said.

I helped her finish the eggnog, while Giles polished off his breakfast. Then, Granny went back to her room to rest. Giles and I were preparing to go for a walk so I could show him the place, when we heard a commotion on the verandah.

The front door swung open, and my cousin Addy swept in. "Sam!" Her eyes lit up. "You come here and give me a big hug."

As I wrapped my arms around her and squeezed, the Mongol horde rushed in around us. The noise level made my ears ache. I had forgotten just how loud the Binks brood could be. I released Addy and held out a hand to Hobart. He wrung my hand 'til I thought my arm would come off.

"Sam, how the hell are you?"

"Doing fine, Hobart. And you?"

His ruddy face beamed. "Pretty dang good."

"Glad to hear it. Addy, Hobart, let me introduce my partner, Giles Blitherington."

Giles stepped forward. Addy and Hobart weren't quite sure what to make of him, but they handled it pretty well. Then came the moment I had been waiting for, the introduction of the three sets of Binks twins. "Giles, these two are the eldest, Bilbo and Frodo."

Giles's head jerked, and he stared at me, no doubt wondering if he had heard me right. The eldest twins, about twenty-eight, offered their hands to Giles. About six feet tall and built like linebackers, Bilbo and Frodo were identical twins. They no longer dressed exactly the same, I was glad to see, but were otherwise hard to tell apart. They had the same haircut, and both wore beards.

"And this is Boromir and Faramir," I said, waving a hand toward the middle set of twins. They were also identical twins, and they were taller and thinner than Bilbo and Frodo.

Giles eyed me as if I were playing some elaborate joke on him, but he greeted the middle twins with his usual aplomb.

"And these two scamps," I said, an arm around the shoulder of each one, "are Arwen and Aragorn." The only pair of the three who were fraternal twins, they were nineteen. Arwen, a sloe-eyed beauty with a voluptuous figure, batted her eyelashes playfully at Giles. As did Aragorn, I noted with interest. I wondered if Addy and Hobart had realized that their youngest son was gay.

The introductions complete, all the twins felt free to resume their conversations. Again the noise level rose. Hobart sent them back outside to unload the car, and he and Addy followed Giles and me into the kitchen. I whispered into Giles's ear that Hobart and Addy were both huge Tolkien fans, which explained the names of their children. He just shook his head.

We had a million things to catch up on. Giles and I told them about life in England, while Hobart talked about the success of his car dealership in Grenada. Addy gave us all the news of the twins' exploits. Bilbo and Frodo were working for their father, while Boromir and Faramir were both in law school at Tulane. Arwen and Aragorn were sophomores at Ole Miss and having the times of their lives while still making top grades.

Loud screeches suddenly rent the air. Addy and Hobart rolled their eyes at each other, and Addy pushed back from the kitchen table. "Lurleen," she said. "She can't stand our kids. She's jealous because her own kids never come to see her. Imagine that."

Lurleen's tirade was running full steam ahead by the time we reached the parlor. Frankly, I had to wonder where she had learned some of the words she was using. Certainly not from Clem or Granny. Maybe from her own kids, who no doubt had told her what they thought of her on more than one occasion.

Lurleen was objecting to the fact that Frodo had turned on the TV to watch a football game. The noise was making her ill, she complained. Intent on the game, Bilbo and Frodo were ignoring her, no doubt out of long habit. Arwen and Aragorn were openly laughing at her tirade, while Boromir and Faramir were each so absorbed in a book that they paid no attention to anything.

Addy cut through the loud vituperation. "Shut up, Lurleen! Just shut the hell up."

Lurleen shut up, her mouth still hanging open.

"If you can't stand to be around the family," Addy said, "then just take your sorry ass upstairs to your bedroom. This is Granny's house, not yours, and we are her guests. If you don't like that, go somewhere else."

"It's going to be my house soon enough," Lurleen said. "The old woman's gonna leave this house to Clem, and once that happens, ain't none of you ever setting foot in this house again."

"Lurleen, honey!" Clem had also come running. "What are you saying?"

"You heard what I said." Lurleen folded her arms across her chest. "I can't wait until this house is ours and I can finally get some peace."

Addy had advanced on the couch and stood glaring down at her sister-in-law. "Listen to me, Lurleen. We've all had enough out of you. Your own children won't even speak to you, you treat your husband like a slave, and you're a total embarrassment to this family. This is my home, and my children's home, as much as it is Clem's, and if we want to come here, we will. You got that?"

Lurleen burst into tears. "Clem, why do you let her talk to me like that? You know it's bad for my heart. I think I'm having a heart attack right now."

Clem had scurried to her side. Addy reached for the nearly full pitcher of water on the table beside Lurleen's couch, lifted it, and poured the entire contents over Lurleen's head.

"Addy," Clem protested weakly as he wiped water from his own face. Lurleen just wailed.

Addy didn't say a word to her brother. She stared at Lurleen.

"I'll get you for this, Addy," Lurleen said. "You wait and see if I don't."

Clem helped Lurleen up from the couch, and the two of them limped out.

"Way to go, Mom!" Aragorn tried to high-five his mother, but she shook her head.

"I just can't take it any more," Addy said. "That woman has made my brother's life a total hell, and she's doing her best to spread that to everyone else. I'll strangle her myself before she keeps me or my family out of this house."

Hobart reached an arm around Addy's shoulders. "Don't let that woman get to you, sweetheart. You know she's mostly hot air anyway."

"I just wish she'd get so full of herself she'd explode and put us out of our misery," Addy said.

"At least you stand up to her," I said. "If Clem had done that years ago, he wouldn't be stuck with such a harpy wife."

Addy sighed. "My brother was born to be a doormat, unfortunately. And he picked a woman who enjoys walking all over him. That's the hell of it."

"We could take her far enough out in the woods and tie her to a tree, where no one'd hear her," Boromir said. Faramir nodded enthusiastically.

Addy laughed. "If it were that simple, I'd do it in a flash. Then Clem could have some kind of life, and his poor kids could actually spend time with their father."

"Now, y'all just hush that kind of talk," Hobart said. "This is Christmas eve, and I don't want to hear any more."

Boromir and Faramir didn't appear too abashed at their father's words. Frankly, I rather liked their idea and would have been willing to help, but I could see Hobart's point.

"Maybe she'll stay upstairs the rest of the day and let us all have some peace." Addy turned and headed for the door. "Time I started on lunch. Aragorn, you and Arwen come help me."

Giles and I followed her and the youngest twins back to the kitchen, while Hobart and the others remained in the parlor to watch the football game.

Addy busied herself with preparations for lunch, setting Aragorn and Arwen to work. I noticed, with great amusement, that Aragorn took every opportunity to get close to Giles and smile at him. At one point, Addy and I exchanged glances. She knew, all right, and didn't seem too bothered by it.

We spent several happy hours in the kitchen, chatting and working away. Hobart and the other twins wandered in and out, looking for beer and munchies. Granny joined us, gliding in on her little chariot, as she called her wheelchair.

The rest of the day proceeded without incident. Lurleen stayed upstairs in her bedroom. Clem appeared now and then, and sometimes we could get him to stay with us for a little while. But he never could relax completely and would soon cast his eyes toward the ceiling. Lurleen would no doubt make him pay for spending those few minutes away from her.

Giles, meanwhile, had a good time with the family. They accepted him, and that pleased me. I had wondered how they would all react, but his own natural charm made it all very easy.

During lunch, Granny asked what all the commotion had been about. Aragorn regaled her with a highly colored account of the argument between his mother and his aunt. Granny simply shook her head. "That woman."

Then she changed the subject, and we moved on to more pleasant topics.

After lunch, Giles and I took took our walk in the bracing December air, while the others napped. We spent a pleasant hour rambling around the property as I showed Giles all the places I had played as a child.

Later that afternoon, we began decorating the parlor for Christmas. Bilbo and Frodo had gone out and found a tree somewhere on the property, a beautiful pine, and it was magnificent by the time we had finished decorating it. I had spent so many Christmases in this house, and I was glad now to share this one with Giles.

After dinner, we played games in the parlor, having a merry old time. Clem appeared now and then, but Lurleen never showed her face. Granny had gone off to rest after dinner but reappeared shortly before midnight. "Just about time for eggnog," she said. It was family tradition that we drink our eggnog around the tree at midnight, singing carols, hailing Christmas Day.

Addy and I followed Granny's whirring wheelchair into the kitchen, where we prepared the eggnog. We used the cups from Granny's best china service. There were twelve, one for each of us, excepting Lurleen. As she desired, her portion was poured into an ugly plastic mug, not the ware used by everyone else.

After Granny sprinkled ground nutmeg into each cup, she directed Addy to carry the full serving tray into the parlor. But she asked me to take Lurleen's cup upstairs to her. "And see if you can't get Clem to come down for just a little while," she said. "Lurleen probably won't come, but he ought to have a few minutes with the family."

"I'll do my best," I told her. I went upstairs, and as I walked down the hall towards Lurleen's room, I glanced down into the plastic mug. I could smell the rum that gave Granny's eggnog such a kick. A few sips of this, and even Lurleen ought to relax a bit.

I stopped for a moment, staring at the ground nutmeg floating on the top of the eggnog. There was something about it . . .

I shook my head. Time to deliver the eggnog and get back downstairs.

I knocked on the door, and Clem called, "Come in."

"Eggnog delivery," I said as I opened the door.

Clem sat in a chair beside the bed. Lurleen was sitting up in the bed, stuffing her face with chocolates.

"Here's your eggnog, Lurleen," I said, handing it to her. She glared at me but took the mug.

"Clem, why don't you come downstairs for a few minutes," I said. "We've got a cup of eggnog for you. You can sing a carol or two with us."

Clem turned to look at his wife. "Would you mind, honey? I won't be gone long." The pleading in his voice angered me. He shouldn't have to live like this.

"Oh, go on," Lurleen said. "Just don't stay too long. I might need you."

"Come on, Clem," I said.

He headed out the door. I was right behind him but turned and looked back at Lurleen. "Drink up, Lurleen. Enjoy your eggnog."

She already had the mug up to her mouth. She flapped one hand at me, telling me to go away. I waited a moment, watching. She gulped down half the eggnog and smacked her lips. Satisfied, I closed the door and went downstairs.

Clem was sitting next to Addy, holding his cup. "Silent Night" filled the air. The twins all had good strong voices, and the beauty of the old carol enveloped us all.

I knelt on the floor beside Granny. She reached out a hand to me, and I grasped it. Her cold hand trembled.

"Did Lurleen drink any of her eggnog?" she asked.

"Yes," I said. "She downed at least half of it before I left the room."

"Good."

"I thought Lurleen was allergic to peanuts," I said.

Granny went completely still for a moment, then she turned her head to look at me. "She is. Deathly allergic."

I nodded. "I guess I ought to keep Clem down here as long as I can."

"That would be a good thing," Granny said. "Poor boy. I can't do much for him, but I do what I can."

"It'll be a shock for a while, but I bet he'll recover pretty quickly."

"I believe he will," Granny said. "I sure hope he will." She turned her head away from me, and I knew she was crying. I held her hand and watched Clem, his arm around his sister, happily singing with the rest of the family.

"Merry Christmas, Clem," I said softly. "Merry Christmas."

DEAN JAMES is the author of eight mystery novels, four of which feature urbane vampire sleuth Simon Kirby-Jones. With Jean Swanson, he is the Macavity and Agatha Award-winning coauthor of *By A Woman's Hand* (Berkley Prime Crime), which was also nominated for the Edgar Award for Best Critical/Biographical Work. Their most recent collaboration is *The Dick Francis Companion* (Berkley Prime Crime). With Elizabeth Foxwell, he is coauthor of *The Robert B. Parker Companion* (Berkley Prime Crime, November 2005). When not writing or reading mysteries, he serves as manager of Murder by the Book in Houston, one of the nation's oldest and largest mystery bookstores.

THE YEAR
BOBBY DO-WOP
WHACKED SANTA

Shelley Fraser Mickle

his story doesn't have anything to do with me. I want to get that out in the open right off. No, this story happened to a friend of mine—Dee Dee Dupree and this boy named Bobby, whose last name I will not reveal even now. In the years that I knew him, we called him Bobby Do-Wop because he was the coolest kid in the sixth grade in a cotton town of fifteen hundred people in flat, dusty Arkansas in the mid 1950s, when an Elvis hairdo and a black leather jacket could get you labeled as irretrievable white trash headed for the state pen.

In the 1950s, fathers were loveable lumps in an armchair with white doily-like antimacassars in the front room. Our sweet mothers didn't keep their mouths exactly shut, but they weren't allowed to say everything they thought, either. And they didn't have jobs outside the house unless they had an uncontrollable passion to teach school or were widows—bless their hearts—or had been dumped in a broken marriage, shame on them. In the latter case, it meant they may not have kept a clean house or cooked enough or, worst of all, "they had let themselves go." (No need to say where. Everyone knew the missing words were "to pot," which didn't have anything to do with smoking or gardening.)

And kids had a lot more freedom than they do today, what with 1950s fathers interpreting their roles as providers and sitting around like steady rocks as role models, though the label "role model" was not yet on tongues. But certainly fathers were not daily confidants. And mothers weren't likely to be driving you all over Kingdom Come, because in those days you could pretty much ride a bike or walk anywhere you wanted to go since there were no outright child molesters or kidnappers, which was really a good thing, seeing as how nobody's parents had enough money for therapy or ransom.

The point is, there was room for secrets.

And boy, do I mean secrets. Heavy, lowdown, wonderful secrets were kept between us kids. Like Sissy White, who accidentally stole Mayor Tiddle's cat, Precious, (it followed her home and she fell in love with it) and then hid it in her bedroom closet for two weeks until it died of diarrhea. We had a secret funeral for it down at the Mill Pond and then went home with Sissy to wash out her closet with Lysol. (Mayor Tiddle, on the chance you are reading this, Precious is on the right-hand corner of the north bank of the Mill Pond near that big magnolia tree—and we want you to know, too, she didn't suffer long.)

And though we were keeping about a million other secrets about each other, that was the only secret about Sissy we'd had to keep so far. For five years she'd kept her nose clean and had grown into a tall, slender upper-elementary school kid with yellow hair curling like scrambled eggs around her heart-shaped face. She was already heading for the cheerleading team because she was double-jointed and could not only do a backbend all the way to get her hands flat on the grass but could also come back up a little way on her front side and wave through her legs.

Sissy was emotional and registered every one of her feelings with her mouth. She could go from a pucker to a grimace, or from biting her lip to extending it toward you in a second flat. Sometimes we didn't know exactly what Sissy's mouth movements meant, but her lips were rarely still. And she was mean in a quiet way. Like the year she was collecting for Easter Seals—she put each one of us in a hammerlock until we dropped a nickel in the contribution jar.

Our biggest secret, though, unbeknownst to anybody over the age of twelve, was that all us kids had switchblade knives. See, we'd gotten into playing a game called "stretch." The rules were that you threw your knife down in the mud (and boy, did it make a great sound, like *thud* or *whack*, depending on the water content of the mud), and your opponent had to stretch a leg to reach it. You kept going that way until you stretched your opponent out, so he or she had to do the splits in the mud, or else cry uncle.

We never carried our switchblades around, but hid them in a cardboard box in an empty railroad car on 3rd Street. (And I would appreciate it if you would not let this out to anyone, because that same boxcar is where Bobby Barnett hid Mrs. Clower's bra after he stole it off her clothesline, and there's no point in her knowing that now, since he married her daughter.)

The big point is, our knives were for play, and so far as our parents knew, none of us kids seemed capable of dark doings.

In some ways, we raised ourselves. We were like weeds, roadside and indigenous, destined to be tough and lasting. And it was ironic that the parenting books of the time even talked about us as foliage—the popular child-raising theory was that "as the tree is bent, so shall it grow." Lucky for us, none of our parents had horticultural aspirations in the first place.

So that's how Bobby Do-Wop was able to give Petey Dupree, Dee Dee's four-year-old brother, a bona fide clinical depression on December 8, 1954, when he told him that Santa Claus was dead.

Petey, no dummy, even at four, looked up at Bobby Do-Wop and said, "You're fudging me." (No, this is not a sanitized version. Kids really talked like this back then.)

"No, I'm not," Bobby Do-Wop replied, and then went on. "Whacked by two elves."

We were standing in the alley between Dee Dee Dupree's house and mine. Petey looked around. No doubt he was searching for Dee Dee as a protector. But she was still in the house polishing her shoes. Dee Dee had a thing about shoes. She had saddle oxfords in three colors. So then Petey looked at each one of us, desperate for someone to come forward to say Bobby was just making up a mean story. But I have to tell the truth now: we didn't say squat. Nobody even made eye contact. We didn't want to mess with Bobby Do-Wop, that was one thing, but we also had flimsy character, no sense of moral obligation whatsoever. And to top it all off, one of us smelled bad, and we were all sniffing around on the sly, trying to discover who it was.

In some ways, I think this was helpful to Petey. It was up to him now to stand up to a bully alone, which everyone always says will eventually strengthen you, if you don't lose consciousness.

"How do you know?" Petey asked, squinting his eyes at Bobby Do-Wop. No bigger than a cocker spaniel standing on its hind legs, Petey had eyes the color of new denim and hair the shade of bicycle rust.

"Let's just say I have my sources," Bobby Do-Wop said. He was making a yo-yo "walk the dog" flawlessly, without so much as cutting an eye at Petey. This is the kind of meanness a tornado owns, barreling through a town without even looking back. We all predicted that when Bobby Do-Wop got old enough to get his driver's license, he would run over somebody and call it a speed bump.

He added for effect, "The elves got into a fight about overtime pay. Santa was playing favorites. Everybody in the toy shop said he got what he deserved. Was hit with a .45 straight through the heart. Bled to death on the doll room floor. So I'm tellin' ya, ya little dirt bag, you ain't gittin' nothin' for Christmas this year. No one is."

I have to hand it to Petey. He held onto his tears longer than a bad cold. He turned with a stoic set to his shoulders and walked into the house. On the way, he passed Dee Dee coming out. He soulfully repeated what Bobby had just told him, then continued into his bedroom, shutting the door behind him. Dee Dee marched straight up to Bobby Do-Wop in her freshly polished saddle oxfords with a little white smudged on the soles, looked him in the eye, and said, "I'm gonna kill you."

Bobby walked his yo-yo for a few seconds on the alley dirt, then pulled it up in a wrist snap and said, "Oh, yeah, I wanna see that."

"Well, you won't see it," Dee Dee Dupree said, " 'cause when I get you, it'll be when you least expect it. I'll give you no warning. I'll flatten you like road kill under a Cadillac."

"Oh, yeah? More, more," Bobby Do-Wop said.

Dee Dee didn't waver. "I'll pop you like a balloon floating down on a spike fence."

"More, more, Miss Dee Dee Diddle-Head, dirt bag in sissy shoes."

"I'll twist your head off your neck in the picture show. You're about to be fed as swill to ravenous pigs, Bobby Do-Wop. Count on it."

Dee Dee's words hissed into the air and chilled us to the bone. We all knew she could mete out vigilante justice, like the time she put raccoon poop on Lester Thompson's bicycle seat after he stole her crayons in Vacation Bible School.

That Saturday afternoon, after declaring Santa Claus dead, Bobby Do-Wop won every game of stretch down at the Mill Pond. He would never play against Dee Dee, though, even when she called him a lily-livered douche bag. He walked home curling his yo-yo around his wrist, making it go "around the world." And we went home muddy and curious. Would Dee Dee really do Bobby in? (We wouldn't have held it against her if she did.)

Bobby had busted one of the most universal secrets, the one that decent people everywhere chip in on every Christmas for the sake of the youngest. I believed there was a special place in Hell for folks who squeeze the magic out of Christmas for little kids. And one day, no doubt, Bobby would be down there yo-yoing for eternity, and with nary a cold Coke.

For two weeks, Petey wouldn't come out of his room. He wouldn't speak or cry for love, money, ice cream, or fireworks. In a moment when his parents weren't watching, I offered him a new switchblade. Instead, he moped around with a sadness not seen since Bambi hit the silver screen. Then on December 12, Mr. and Mrs. Dupree drove Petey to a specialist in Little Rock.

The Duprees had to sit a long time in the waiting room, since seven other families from our little town were there, too. All had the same complaint and got the same eventual diagnosis: Holiday Associated Childhood Depression. Also known as the Dead Santa Claus Blues.

But not one of the little kids, not even Julie Wilson, who fell on the floor in the doctor's office and spoke in tongues, would point a finger at Bobby Do-Wop. He had gone through town telling every kid under the age of five that Santa Claus had been cremated on July 25 and his ashes spread on rooftops from here to Abilene, Texas. (Why Abilene, I'm not sure, except that Bobby Do-Wop once sent off a cereal box top to Abilene for a prize, and, as he said, "Didn't win nothing.") And here was the clinker: Bobby set up news of Santa's death like a chain letter, so once you heard about it, you had to pass it on. He told little kids if they stopped the oral chain letter, some kind of bad luck like an ingrown toenail or life-long constipation would befall them. And not only that, but any kid who mentioned Bobby Do-Wop's name in connection with Santa's oral obituary would then have to answer to Bobby Do-Wop's switchblade.

It was clear we bigger kids had to step in and do something to resurrect Santa. But we were having a hard time agreeing how. Billy Barnes wanted Santa to have a long list of sons who could inherit his job. Junior Timmons wanted Santa to be raised from the dead like Lazarus by Jesus, but he was holding out for Rudolph to play the part of Jesus. Sissy White wanted Santa to have been wearing a bulletproof vest. (Personally I liked her version best.) Meanwhile, none of us was saying what really was a side necessity—that Bobby Do-Wop needed to be taken out. And then, in the week before Christmas, just as we'd been secretly wishing it, Bobby Do-Wop disappeared.

Initially, we thought it was a natural rebalancing of the world, like God flooding the land and letting Noah float off with the good parts. But then, Mrs. Wilson found Bobby Do-Wop's bike torn apart under the water tower. And there were drops of what looked like blood on the saddle.

Mr. Lane spied Bobby Do-Wop's leather jacket turned inside out with the zipper torn off in the back row of the picture show.

Sissy White found a tuft of Bobby's telltale VO5 hair on the gym floor. She turned it over to the sheriff, who put it away as possible criminal evidence.

Lucille Betts, the kooky school librarian, suggested that Bobby had been carted off by wolves. She said his books were always overdue, and whenever they did come back they looked chewed by wolves. Likely, he'd been hanging out with a pack for some time.

Then the sheriff arrested Bobby's dad. Mr. Do-Wop was an incurable drunk who'd beaten Bobby's mother until she could no longer hide it under Band-Aids. She had run off long ago, when Bobby was a mere babe. Generally speaking, Mr. Do-wop was rarely home awake.

On the sixth day before Christmas, we traipsed through the jail to peek at Bobby's father behind the bars. Dirty, pickled with alcohol, red-faced, and splotch-nosed to the point of looking like a stewed tomato, he sure appeared mean and capable of murder, as well as pitiful. Mrs. Betts organized a cakewalk for the benefit of Bobby. She wanted to raise funds for his funeral; that is, if his body was ever found. If not, the funds would go to the library.

Meanwhile, the sheriff tried to find out if Mr. Do-Wop had taken out that school insurance on Bobby at the first of the year. That school insurance promised you five thousand dollars if you lost a thumb on the playground, four thousand for an ear, and ten thousand for a whole body. That insurance could be a motive. It was taking the school a good while to hunt up Bobby's insurance form, though. (Because in those days, you had to file through stuff with a rubber thimble on your thumb.)

Meanwhile, we kids were in a moral pickle. Should we let Bobby's father fry when we knew that Dee Dee Dupree had threatened Bobby with murder? From what we knew about Dee Dee, it wasn't hard to believe she had followed through. She was the following-through kind, you know, a straight-A kind of kid. She never had books overdue and had that fussy type of personality, always picking lint off your collar.

Should we, shouldn't we?

Tell, don't tell?

Let good old Dee Dee get away with murder for the rest of her squeaky-clean life, or serve her up on a silver platter?

We turned these questions over and over in every game of stretch. We waited for our switchblades to give us some kind of sign that we could read. *Whack*, into the mud with a switchblade to ask, "Turn Dee Dee over?" And then *thud*, "Keep Dee Dee's secret forever?"

Then, Sissy White came up to me after school on the fourth day before Christmas and pursed her lips. "Wanna see something?"

Now, I will say, since this is not really incriminating evidence, I have never been able to turn down a Hershey bar or a chance to see something.

So I followed Sissy to the edge of town. We trudged through a cotton field and walked through a dry ditch. She took me to a shack that had recently been a busy chicken coop. Its doors and windows were closed up, and when she said, "Here, stand here," I did as I was told. She knocked on the boarded-up window three times. Right away, a long finger with a chewed-off nail and a bloody-looking cuticle came sticking out of a crack. Sissy reached in her pocket and took out a package of Junior Mints. She took one mint out of the box and stuck it on the end of the finger. The finger disappeared back inside the shack, and I heard a smacking noise.

And then a voice: "More, more."

After two more mints were put on that pitiful-looking finger, followed up by short suck on a straw from a bottle of Grape Nehi, I realized I'd heard that voice say "more, more," somewhere else at another time but in a much different tone. Yes, Sissy White was holding Bobby Do-Wop inside the shack, just like she'd held the mayor's cat in her closet. I wondered if she'd fed Precious a diet of Junior Mints, too.

"Sissy," I said. "You have to let him out."

"Why?" She looked at me with her doll eyes. Her question sat in the air a good while.

Yes, the existential nature of that question did appeal to me, and at another time I might have argued it for a good long while. But at the moment, I was worried about the fact that my grandmother had recently bought twenty-four chickens out of that chicken coop, and all two dozen were in her freezer waiting for our family Sunday dinners that we always had right after church. I didn't think I could eat one more of those chickens knowing that Bobby Do-Wop's shriveled, murdered body was decomposing on the exact spot where my dinner had come from.

So I did what I knew I had to do. I grabbed Sissy's right hand, twirled it around her back in a hammerlock, kicked open the chicken house door, and cried, "Run, Bobby, run!"

For a second he crouched on the floor laden with chicken poop, and then he sprang out the door and into the woods like a possum caught in the middle of daylight. He was running so fast, I got a feeling he wouldn't stop for a good while.

"For godsakes let go of me," Sissy was saying.

That was simple enough. I did.

She didn't hold anything against me. She just did one of her famous backbends in the grass to wipe her hands clean of the melted chocolate and to get the kinks out of her arm from where I'd held it. We walked back to town, finishing up the box of Junior Mints, and we never breathed a word that we knew anything at all about Bobby Do-Wop, other than that we thought one day he might reappear.

The town put on a real bang-up cakewalk. Four hundred dollars were raised for Bobby's funeral. His father was taken to the next county, where the public defender hoped he could receive a fair trial. And on December 24, Lucille Betts opened up the library and began cleaning the shelves. With no body to bury, the place was going to get refurbished real soon. Even the principal was excited.

But on Christmas morning, as all the town's little kids were waking up, finding a piddling little something under the Christmas tree as they always did, Bobby Do-Wop and his dad came strutting into town. Bobby had on a new leather jacket, and he had a coupon for every kid in town. He placed printed cards on everyone's doors: *Here, take this to Mrs. Betts and ask for some of my burial money. Then buy whatever you want that you didn't get. P.S. Santa Claus ain't dead. He's just sick of Christmas. I saw him last week, hiding out at the edge of town. He's good for next year. Merry Christmas, you little dirt bags.*

Now, since I'm telling this, I might add here that if there's a moral to this story, it probably has to do with the power of chicken coops and the quiet sense of justice harbored within little blonde girls. Beware, too, of those who can do extraordinary backbends. And pass on the word: Santa lives.

SHELLEY FRASER MICKLE is a novelist and public radio commentator. Her first novel, *The Queen of October*, was a *New York Times* Notable Book, and her second, *Replacing Dad* became a CBS movie. Her most recent novel, *The Turning Hour*, is being taught in many north Florida high schools. Her radio essays have been collected under the title, *The Kids Are Gone; The Dog Is Depressed & Mom's on the Loose*. She has been reading her essays on NPR's *Morning Edition* since 2000 and is frequently heard on *Recess*, a public radio program produced at the University of Florida.

Secret Santa

Sarah Shankman

It was the first Friday after Thanksgiving break, the day when the members of the English department at Atlanta's Piedmont High chose names for Secret Santa. And despite the fact Beth knew what she knew—that Nadia was toast—she held her breath as Nadia drew the first slip of paper from the brown paper bag.

"If you pick Beth, we'll definitely know the fix is in," said Big Bob, who played Santa at their party every year. "Four times in four years? Gimme a break. It's no fair always picking your best friend." The odds of Nadia's picking Beth's name again were only one in thirteen—no, make that twelve. If Nadia pulled her own name from the bag, she would have to put it back.

Nadia flashed a quick smile. "I've always been lucky," she said. "Maybe I should be buying Powerball tickets." Then she laughed after silently reading the name on her slip of paper.

"Oh, no!" cried Agnes, their department chair. "Not again."

Nadia shook her head, grinning, then ran a thumb and forefinger across her lips. Zipped.

Both Agnes and Big Bob ought to know better. Beth had tried to tell them about Nadia. But so be it. This time would be different, no matter how Nadia engineered the drawing.

I'm loaded for bear this time, she thought. Do your worst, Nadia. The jig is up.

No one noticed the set of Beth's chin and her determined gaze, despite the long narrow office's being especially jammed this day with the English department's baker's dozen, plus a handful of other faculty who hung out with them. And had anyone commented, Beth would have shrugged and said, "Oh, it's just Friday. Busy week." But she wanted to shout Nadia's transgressions. Oh, how she'd love to fling the C-word at Nadia's head, and she didn't mean Christmas. But it was important to maintain a front of civility; they all had to get along.

"It's just your imagination. I don't know what you mean." That was Nadia's answer each time Beth had confronted her this past year.

It hadn't always been this way. Their first two years at Piedmont, she and Nadia, both in their late twenties, had been the tightest of pals and all of Nadia's gifts a sheer delight. It was only when their friendship went south that Secret Santa had become one more opportunity for Nadia to cut Beth to the quick. She could imagine Nadia's saying, "Oh, Agnes, let me do that," printing everyone's name, then marking Beth's with a crimp.

But this year, Beth had a secret weapon up her sleeve.

CHRISTMAS WAS ALWAYS A bad time for Beth McFarland. Night after December night she was ripped from sleep by her mother's shout of *Frank, watch out!* cutting like a fire engine's wail across the sweet strains of "Silent Night" on her father's truck radio.

Beth had been nine, that last happy Christmas season, and in orbit with excitement. Santa, a.k.a. Mom and Dad, were going to give her—fingers crossed, she just knew it—the bicycle she'd spied when shopping with her mother one day in nearby Athens. Pink with purple trim and confetti-like silver streamers hanging from the handlebars, it was the bike of Beth's dreams. None of her friends in Elberton had anything remotely as wonderful.

"You're looking awfully red-cheeked," her mom had teased as they'd stood at the edge of Elberton's town square waiting for the annual lighting of the tree. Brilliant with lights and scarlet bows, the massive white pine towered above the statue of the Confederate soldier. Mom laid a cool hand on her only child's forehead. "Are you sure you don't have a fever?"

Pink-bicycle fever, Beth had thought.

Her best friend, Linda, had told her that you could name your heart's delight—the thing that you really truly wanted above all else—only once. Any more than that, you'd rub the shiny off and it would escape your grasp. "Like my dad," Linda said, "when he was hoping for that promotion at the quarry. He kept talking about that promotion and what he was going to do with the raise. My mom tried to shush him, but he wouldn't stop. She didn't say I told you so when they gave the job to Mr. Burton instead, but I could tell she was thinking it."

So Beth kept quiet about the amazing pink bike.

"If you're coming down with something, maybe we ought to skip making cookies this evening," her mom had said, a twinkle in her eye.

"No! I'm not sick!" Beth insisted.

So bake they did. Beth's mom adored making holiday treats: sand tarts, maple roll-ups, lemon loves, snickerdoodles, lizzies for just a bite of fruitcake, cheese straws, candied pecans, gingerbread men, and sugar cookies dusted with red and green sanding sugar and silver dragées. They'd made pecan, pumpkin, and mincemeat pies and a yellow layer cake with cocoa icing, just for fun. Plus, as always, at her daddy's request, a big pan full of her mom's secret-recipe brownies.

Then they'd decked the house to the strains of the round-the-clock Christmas music station, hanging silver globes, golden bows, ropes of tinsel, and Beth's mom's collection of precious Christmas ornaments, several passed down from her grandmother, ever so fragile, nearly a hundred years old. They'd placed electric candles in every window of their two-story colonial house. And Beth's dad had made plans to add to the display of yard lights.

"I'll take off early and we'll run over to Athens this afternoon to Pastime Hardware," Beth's dad had said to her mother one morning a week before Christmas. "I want to do the shrubbery with those icicle lights I told you about."

Athens! They were going to get her bike! She'd stood very still. *Please, please,* she petitioned the heavens.

"We'll be leaving before you get home from school, Beth," said Mom. "So you go next door to Aunt Helen's when school's out, and we'll pick you up after supper."

"OK." Beth had arranged her face into careful neutrality. She wasn't fond of her stiff Aunt Helen, as different from her warm, funny mother as apples from oranges. Mom was the baby of their family of ten; Aunt Helen, the oldest. Helen's own two boys were already grown and long gone.

"As soon as they could get out of the house," Beth had once overheard Daddy saying, but Mom had shushed him. "Helen means well," she insisted. "She never got to be a child, really, helping raise the rest of us."

Beth had been on pins and needles all that afternoon, fidgeting over her homework in Aunt Helen's kitchen, which smelled of Lysol and bleach. It was difficult to concentrate over Aunt Helen's constant stream of complaints. Stuck up, was her opinion of her minister's wife. "I don't see why. It's not as if they're not beholden to us for every bite of food they put in their mouths." Nor was she happy with her sons' Christmas plans. "Only dropping by here on Christmas Eve so the kids can pick up their presents, seems to me."

Uncle Jack had cleared his throat but didn't say anything to that. "Couldn't get a word in edgewise if he tried," was Daddy's opinion about him.

"They ought to be home by now," Uncle Jack had said, frowning into his gold pocket watch at seven-thirty.

"Probably all those presents." Aunt Helen's mouth had been tight with disapproval. "They spoil you-know-who rotten."

By nine o'clock the house had grown silent, every ear alert for the sound of tires in the driveway. When the phone had rung at ten-thirty, they all sprang for it, Helen reaching it first. It was the Georgia State Patrol, she'd said white-faced and mouthing the words from the receiver to Uncle Jack as if Beth couldn't see. After that, the details of the head-on crash that killed her parents would always be a blur to Beth.

In her nightmares there were lightning-like flashes of clarity: a narrow dark road, the swerving headlights of the drunk driver crossing the yellow line, their Christmas presents littering a field. Later, the white roses her mother so loved blanketing the coffins like thick snow.

Beth's pink bike had been unscathed in its sturdy box, but she didn't want it, never saw it. Later Uncle Jack told her it had gone to a poor child in another town, far away. He'd wanted to make sure she'd never stumble upon it.

EVERY YEAR THEREAFTER, with the approach of Christmas, Beth felt her chest tighten. Aunt Helen and Uncle Jack, with whom she'd gone to live, had never known quite what to do about the holidays. Some years they did too little, others too much. As a child, it had never occurred to Beth that the holidays would be tough for them, too.

Just after Thanksgiving, her freshman year at Emory in Atlanta, Beth had fallen into a black hole of depression. "We're going for help," her roommate, Liz, had insisted, pulling her out of bed. The campus therapist had advised, "Don't push yourself. If being in Elberton's too tough, don't go, or go for just a day. Hold onto a few rituals; let the rest go without apology. Invent new rituals that make you feel good."

So that was how Beth and Liz began their annual Christmas cookie parties. They decorated a tree with Beth's mother's ornaments, made a big pot of chili, and invited their girlfriends over to bake cookies. Though sometimes tears welled as Beth pulled out her mother's cookie cutters, the aromas of vanilla and butter and sugar baking and the laughter of women working together in the kitchen made her happy.

Her first Christmas at Piedmont, several of her fellow English teachers had joined in the fun: Agnes, Louise, and Anne, the old guard of the department; and Nadia, Jill, and Joanna, the new hires along with Beth.

Nadia's cookies had been the hit of that afternoon. One batch, perfect miniature stained glass windows. Another, silvery snowflakes. Not that anyone was suprised; already it was clear that Nadia Brooks had a special touch with everything she turned her hand to.

From day one, students had trailed Nadia as if she were a rock star. She danced, she sang in a rich contralto, drew and painted, threw pots, and blew the most amazing glass. Her knowledge of literature seemed boundless, even more impressive because the Ph.D. that she mentioned occasionally was in molecular biology.

Nadia said she'd worked in research in Washington, D.C., for a few years, but when her dad died she, an only child like Beth, had wanted to be closer to her mother, Mimi—who'd once danced with the Paris Ballet. The position at Piedmont High had offered Nadia the chance to teach drama, "my real love."

Beth had been smitten with Nadia at first sight, harboring a crush as if she were a schoolgirl herself rather than the instructor of three sections of sophomore literature and composition and two of junior/senior creative writing. Beth had been flattered when Nadia encouraged their budding friendship.

And a little intimidated. Nadia was sophisticated. Worldly. She spoke French. A little Italian. A "smattering" of Spanish. Growing up, she'd spent summers in France with relatives who'd taken her touring everywhere.

The first time they'd dined together at a little French bistro in Buckhead, Beth was afraid she would embarrass herself. What if she couldn't decipher the menu? Would she have to eat snails or kidneys? She knew nothing about French wine other than that everyone made a big deal about Beaujolais nouveau.

But the menu had been a breeze, and over roasted chicken with an herbed hollandaise Nadia had enthralled her with tales of her mother's family. French Jews, they'd been hidden during World War II by friends in a village near Paris where they'd buried their silver just as Beth's great-great-great-grandmother had done when the Yankees marched through Georgia. "But their art," said Nadia, "they stored that with gentile friends in Paris, and when the war was over, poof!"

"What do you mean?" asked Beth.

"*What art? What Monet? What Picasso drawing?* Their so-called friends pretended they didn't know what my grandpère was talking about."

Monet? Picasso? Beth was speechless.

"But I've been nattering on," twinkled Nadia. "Enough about me. Tell me about your family. Brothers? Sisters? Tell me about Elberton."

"Oh . . . it's . . ." Beth faltered. Her history was so small-town, so terribly dull compared to Nadia's cosmopolitan origins. Elberton, a town of fewer than five thousand souls in northeast Georgia, was the granite capital of the world. Its hundred-plus sheds and manufacturing plants turned rough blocks of granite dug from area quarries into memorials, headstones, and mausoleums. Houses, street markers, and now the local football stadium were finished in granite, giving the whole town a funereal air.

Nevertheless Nadia's skillful questioning had drawn her out, and by the end of the third glass of the lovely rosé that Nadia had suggested, Beth had told her all about her mother and father, their tragic end, and the years with Aunt Helen and Uncle Jack.

"Aunt Helen sounds like a dragon lady," said Nadia shaking her head.

"Oh, she meant well." The years with Aunt Helen hadn't been easy. Whereas her parents had always been ready to laugh and joke, Aunt Helen held opinions. Her displeasure spilled out in torrents of judgment, then dammed into silence. A less-than-perfect report card or a lost book bag would occasion a week of wordless suppers. Home ten minutes late from a date, Beth would find Helen waiting to open and shut the door, her unspoken disappointment ringing in Beth's ears.

"I hate that," said Nadia. "People should spit out what's bothering them and move on. Punishing someone like that is cruel."

"Yes," Beth had nodded, happy to be understood.

"Now," Nadia had said, smoothing the tablecloth. "Tell me about your boyfriends. Are you seeing someone special?"

Beth had shaken her head.

"No? A girl pretty as you?"

Beth's blush had begun just south of her collarbone and spread upwards to the roots of her strawberry blonde hair. She knew she was moderately attractive—average in size and height and with regular features, she had been lucky enough to inherit her mother's good skin, dimples, and delphinium blue eyes. But girls of her ilk were a dime a dozen in the Deep South. A Saturday shopping trip through Lenox Square would tell you that.

Nadia's looks would catch the eye, though. Small, dark, exotic Nadia had a long wolfish face—to Beth's mind, typically French. She wore simple clothes, wonderfully cut, the likes of which Beth never saw anywhere in Atlanta.

"No one who mattered for a while now," Beth had allowed.

Nadia had scooted her chair closer. "Tell me about the last one who did."

Beth couldn't remember the last time she'd talked about Reece Rivers, the pain still fresh a year later. But once she'd started, she couldn't stop. Nadia's dark eyes encouraged her, never leaving her face.

Beth had been a senior in college when a sorority sister said to her, "When my brother comes home from California, you absolutely must meet him." One early spring afternoon, Beth had returned to her dorm to find, lounging on the front steps, a taller, leaner male version of her sorority friend, a campus beauty with dark hair and eyes and rosy cheeks.

"You must be Beth," he'd said, his smile revealing slightly crooked teeth that saved his movie-star looks from being too perfect. Reece had wooed her with roses, a beribboned bottle of Chanel No. 5 left in her mailbox, impassioned conversations over late-night burgers and beer at Manuel's Tavern. During long walks through the shady neighborhoods of North Druid Hills, past wonderful old houses, they would choose first this one, then that, as their imaginary future home.

"But he had moods," Beth had explained. "We'd be in the middle of a conversation, and he'd suddenly grow dark and silent. He'd never tell me what I'd said wrong."

"Sounds like your Aunt Helen."

Beth had stared at Nadia. Why had she never made that connection herself?

Filled with the joyous first flush of a budding friendship, she couldn't confide in Nadia quickly enough. "Nevertheless, I was crazy about Reece.

And always, up to the very last, he talked as if there were no doubt that we had a future together."

"And then he left you for another woman," Nadia had said.

Beth's espresso had stopped halfway to her lips. "How did you know?"

She rarely spoke of that terrible afternoon when Reece had mentioned, as if it were something that had always been understood between them, that he was to be married in a month to a woman back in California. She had excused herself to the bathroom, where she'd hurled her lunch. In the following month she'd rarely slept and dropped fifteen pounds. The thought of him could still make her eyes sting.

"Men," Nadia had shrugged, the world-weariness of generations of French women in that gesture that implied, *Of course he'd jilt you. That's what men do.* Then Nadia had brightened. "But Hank? Maybe he's different, you think?"

Hank? Hank Dawson, their fellow teacher, was a sweetheart of a guy who taught English to low achievers. Hank's Hooligans they were called, many of them stoners fresh out of juvenile hall. Beth had tried to feign innocence, but there was her blush again, giving her away. Was her little crush so obvious? Or was Nadia's nose for human interaction even keener than she'd realized?

Nadia had laughed. "He gives you sly glances when you're not looking. He's awfully shy. You may need to step up to the plate a bit, give him a bit of encouragement. Worth it, I'd think. He is cute." She'd paused. "Reminds me more than a little of Michael."

Nadia had only rarely mentioned the boyfriend who roared into town on his motorcycle and spirited her off to art openings. Once she'd said something about their flying to New York for a weekend. But none of the Piedmont crowd had ever met him. Michael was a painter, Beth had overheard Nadia say, who lived in a cabin he'd built near Jasper, in the Blue Ridge foothills.

Nadia had assured Beth, "Until you and the Hankster get it together, your secret's safe with me."

BUT BETH WAS NEVER one to make the first move, and she and Hank had remained just chums.

Still, by the time of Nadia's student-faculty production of *Midsummer Night's Dream* that marked the end of their first school year, no one else had appeared on her horizon, and Beth, watching Hank in rehearsal, had found herself wondering if she'd been too careful for her own good.

Nadia had cast Beth in a tiny role as Mustardseed, one of the fairies, which suited her just fine. Hank starred as Puck, the court jester and fool. He'd been splendid in the role, funny as could be, loose-limbed, darling, in a word. So who was the fool here? She's thought that maybe she ought to say something to him. Summer was coming; the pressure would be off . . . Except that he and a buddy had been about to leave on a summer-long biking tour of the west. As he'd transformed Bottom's head into that of an ass on stage, Rose Oliveto had slipped into the seat beside Beth, whispering, "He's terrific, isn't he?"

Rose taught senior honors English. She was socially awkward, a bit dumpy, and forever trying to hide her too-prominent nose behind a curtain of long brown curls.

"Hank is good," Beth had agreed, careful to give nothing away. Rose's discretion was questionable at best.

But Rose had other fish to fry. "I would have liked a larger part," she'd said. "I really could have handled more than Tom Snout, you know."

"Well, sure, but this is primarily a student . . ." Beth had trailed off as it dawned on her. Tom Snout. She hadn't made the connection before, but what a perfectly awful role for Rose. Surely Nadia hadn't . . . "I'm sure Nadia would have given you more of a challenge if you'd asked." Then Beth had turned her attention back to the stage, hoping that Rose would do the same.

Rose had grown silent, but when Beth turned to look at her again, she'd seen tears in Rose's big brown eyes.

"No, Nadia wouldn't," Rose had murmured. "Nadia doesn't like me."

Beth had considered Rose a whiner at this point. "Of course she does."

"No, she doesn't. She doesn't include me. I'm not talking about your parties, that kind of thing. I mean just the two of us."

Beth flinched. She'd been so happy to be included, she'd paid no attention to what it might feel like to be Rose, on the outside looking in. But it wasn't as if anyone had set out to exclude Rose specifically. She was nice enough but just didn't fit in. She seemed way older than her years, prissy, and she took offense too easily. Like now.

"Oh, Rose. Of course Nadia likes you."

"She used to. When y'all first came to Piedmont, at the beginning of the year, she was nice to me. We talked, went to dinner together a couple of times, the symphony. And then, all of a sudden, it was over. She gave me the cold shoulder, and when I asked her why, she pretended she didn't know what I meant."

Okay, so Nadia had grown bored with Rose. Face it, Rose was irritating. But Nadia's not speaking to her? That had to be Rose's imagination. "You know," Beth said, "Nadia has been awfully busy with the play."

Rose's eyes had flashed hurt, then anger and resignation before shuttering down completely. "Busy," she'd said, mouth in a tight line. "Sure, she's very busy."

Rose's whining had been embarrassing. It stank of the grammar school playground. Beth had turned her attention back to the stage as Hank completed a turn that left him gasping for breath. His fierce energy was very sexy.

"Bravo!" Nadia had exclaimed, then took the boards herself to stand in for the absent student playing Titania, queen of the fairies. She had that thing, the magic of the born actress.

Her speech: Titania, the fairy queen, scolding her husband for the dalliances that made him ignore the whistling wind they'd once enjoyed together. In revenge, she claimed, the wind had punished them with fog. The pathetic fallacy, Beth had thought, plucking from her grad school days the term for giving human emotions to inanimate objects or nature.

"She lies, too," Rose had hissed as she took her leave. "Nadia makes things up."

Talk about pathetic, Beth had thought.

HANK HAD SENT BETH a couple of postcards from his bicycle trip, and she'd thought, *He'll call when he's back.* But he hadn't. And just before her second year at Piedmont began, she'd met Gene, a friend of Liz, her old college roomie and best nonteacher friend. He was nice but not quite heart-soaring.

Back at school, Hank had greeted her with a huge happy hug, and she'd felt her heart lurch in his direction, but in the weeks soon after he seemed to grow cool. Or maybe that had just been her imagination. For when the gang of school friends who—Gene notwithstanding—had become the center of her social life were all together, Hank had acted pretty much the same as ever.

They'd all spent major time together: parties, softball, bowling as a goof, pizza after school every Friday. There'd been women-only birthday parties, and in the summer, the guys went backpacking. The core group was composed of five men, including Hank, and six women, Nadia among them.

Meanwhile Beth and Nadia's own *pas de deux* had continued. They'd gossiped on the phone, gone to movies and concerts. The route from Beth's apartment in Midtown to the old house Nadia rented in Peachtree Hills had become well worn. They'd exchanged secrets and small presents, Beth adding to Nadia's collections of odd bracelets and jazz CDs, while Nadia kept an eye out for vintage Christmas tree ornaments as well as the kitschy fake food—chocolates, cookies, fruit, replicas of hamburgers—that Beth loved. Beth had heard more stories about Nadia's parents, her mother's dance career, her trips with Michael, though she still hadn't met him or any of them. Nadia was one of those people who keep their lives compartmentalized.

I'm a fortunate woman, Beth had often thought. She'd always miss her parents, of course, but the worst was behind her, except for the December nightmares. Otherwise she was happy in her job, rich with friends, loved her apartment. The relationship with Gene had been sweet if hardly thrilling, and it eventually died a slow but painless death.

Before Beth knew it, another year had rolled around and her third Thanksgiving at Piedmont had been nearly upon her. Then one day Nadia had casually mentioned that Michael was coming for a visit.

"Drop by for coffee," Beth had offered. "I'll make a batch of brownies." Beth had yet to lay eyes on Michael and Nadia was a fool for chocolate; Beth's mom's secret-recipe brownies were among her favorites. "I'll be around most of the weekend."

Nadia had just smiled and said nothing. Nor did she ever call.

THINKING BACK, BETH RECOGNIZED the moment of that unanswered invitation as the line of demarcation. Overnight, where once there'd been a bridge of laughter and affection between herself and Nadia, sly winks across the crowded office at private jokes, long lunches, and happy outings, there yawned a void of silence.

It had taken Beth a while to realize that the friendship was dead. Nadia's not stopping by her classroom, leaving phone calls unreturned, avoiding her eyes in their everyday encounters—at first she had written those all off to her own imagination. Or to Nadia's being distracted or busy. Perhaps Michael's visit hadn't gone well. Maybe her mother was ill.

Yet the day of the Secret Santa drawing, Nadia had been merry as ever, coy about whose name she'd drawn, and she'd, yes, given Beth a wink as if to signal, *You again*. But then she'd retreated, chatty with others, silent toward Beth. That silence stung Beth badly, echoing the long years of Aunt Helen's mute disapproval that had worn deep grooves in her soul.

Then one afternoon, Beth had stepped into the office to copy some tests and stumbled upon Nadia alone. Her first impulse had been to turn on her heel and flee. She wasn't at her best that day, a Christmas nightmare—the dark highway, the headlights crossing the line, the screech of metal—having consumed her sleep the night before. Nevertheless, she'd decided to give Nadia the benefit of the doubt. *She has to know she's made a mistake here. She's embarrassed and doesn't know how to begin the road back.*

Beth had taken a deep breath. "Hey!" she'd breezed. "So, I'll see you at my cookie party Saturday?"

Nadia had shaken her head. "No," she said.

No *sorry*. No *can't*. No *other plans*. Nadia had turned back to the paper she'd been marking.

Then Beth had blurted, "Listen, Nadia. Is anything wrong? Have I said or done something to hurt your feelings? You know I wouldn't—"

"No," Nadia had interrupted. The single word, as before. Her face expressionless.

Beth hadn't been able to stop. "Well, I just, you know, it seems as if you've . . ." Hating herself for explaining, for being apologetic, as if she were the one who'd been neglectful.

Finally, Beth had managed to shut her mouth and do what she should have done in the beginning: flee. Trembling with rage and humiliation, she'd stomped down the hall back to her classroom and slammed the door behind her. "Screw you and the broom you rode in on," she spat into the empy room. "Screw you, Nadia Brooks, you witch."

THE FOLLOWING WEEK HAD found Beth reluctantly pulling on her black satin pants, dressing for the department Christmas party at Agnes's house. Please, God, she thought. Don't let Nadia be my Secret Santa again. I can't fake the gratitude.

Nadia's gifts were always fabulous, and her Secret Santa presents always upped her own ante. The celadon bowl she'd thrown still sat in the middle of Beth's dining table, filled with nuts, oranges, and pomegranates. The sweater she'd knitted from silvery blue yarn, a perfect match for Beth's eyes, had, like the bowl, been greeted with *oohs* and *aahs* of praise.

Now Beth looked at those gifts with new eyes. They were a sort of double dip, weren't they? Grand for the recipient, sure, but didn't they heap glory on Nadia's own head as well?

What, she had wondered, might it be this year, given Nadia's antipathy: a stocking filled with coal, a dead rat, a steaming turd?

No, Nadia was much too clever for something so obvious. Nothing that would tip her hand to others. And the odds were against it anyway. Three times out of three?

Amid the festivities, the pile of Secret Santa presents had dwindled as Bob handed them out one by one. Then, "Beth! Here you go!" Big Bob had passed a beautifully wrapped gift over to her.

All eyes had turned to Nadia, smiling innocently, lovely in a velvet shift of bottle green. Beth's heart had thudded as she ripped the star-scattered gold wrapping paper to reveal the familiar navy blue box beneath.

It had become a joke between the two girlfriends, this box that had first held a pair of purple satin slippers, a birthday present from Beth. Since then the box had passed back and forth between them. *Is it bigger than a shoebox?* had been their running joke.

Then, swaddled in billows of golden tissue paper Beth had found a cerulean blue Christmas tree ornament of blown glass. Around its circumference rode a figure of a tiny blonde, blue-eyed woman astride a bicycle.

A bicycle of an amazing pink.

Beth had felt as if she'd opened a door only to find empty space on the other side. And she'd stepped through and was falling, falling while all around her, her stupid friends sang Nadia's praises: *How precious! Where on earth did you find it? Beth to the very life! You made it?*

Beth's ears had buzzed. How dare she? Nadia knew how devastating that Christmas . . . how guilt had clawed at her for years . . . if only she hadn't wanted the bike . . . if only her mom and dad hadn't driven to Athens that night.

Of course Nadia knew. That had been the point, hadn't it? She'd reached back into Beth's past for a weapon that would cut her to the quick, then swathed the dagger in golden tissue paper.

AFTER THAT EVENING WHEN, to Beth's mind, Nadia moved from passive cruelty to active, she had never looked Nadia's way again unless their workaday routine necessitated an exchange. I'll simply go about my business, she had told herself. I won't let her get to me. Snubbing someone didn't come naturally to Beth. It was creepy, she'd thought, and made her more than a little uncomfortable.

It hadn't been as if she could take comfort from Agnes or any of her other school buddies who might have registered Nadia's coldness toward her and said, *Isn't she awful?* No one saw. No one noticed, for the sheer conviviality of their crowd, the constant chatter, the joking, the cross-talking served as Nadia's smokescreen. They were absolutely brilliant, Nadia's crimes of omission. What she did was nothing, and they were such a happy, wordy bunch that Nadia's behavior was invisible.

Just as, Beth had realized with a jolt, Nadia's silence toward Rose had gone unnoticed.

Poor Rose Oliveto, who after one more miserable year had married her fiancé, George, and moved to Houston. Rose had gathered her nerve and tried to tell Beth about the misery Nadia caused her, and Beth had just blown her off, so smug in her own happiness. Grateful and thrilled to be at the center of their Piedmont gang, basking in the sun of Nadia's special affection.

Beth had flushed at her own pettiness. As bad as her own students, she'd thought, cliquish and petty teenage girls desperate to secure their own spots in the pecking order. And, yet, wouldn't her own peers look at her with dubious eyes if she complained to them?

THE PHONE CALLS HAD begun that spring. In the middle of the night, three, four times, the phone would ring, then nothing but silence on the other end. It hadn't taken long before Beth found herself dreading bedtime, knowing that sooner or later she'd be ripped from sleep to twist in the wind until dawn. She couldn't turn off the phone at night because her Uncle Jack, of all the sweet angels who didn't deserve cancer, wasn't doing well. Not well at all.

Then the pattern had changed. No longer was her hello met with a void but by a young man's voice crooning, *Beth, I know you're lonely, you're always there alone.* . . . Again and again throughout the dark nights, he'd call— sometimes she could hear other young voices in the background—singing lines from the old Kiss song entitled with her name.

Beth had finally confided in Liz. "It's threatening. It's weird."

Liz had agreed, but she didn't understand how the phone calls related to Nadia.

"Back when we were friends, sometimes she'd sing the song as a hello. It was a joke. She knows how to push my buttons. Just like she knows about my nightmares."

"Yeah . . . but these are kids. You think she put them up to it?"

"I know it sounds crazy."

"No, but you haven't had a good night's sleep in how long? And I'm sure Nadia's nastiness is weighing on you. I, of course, would just tell her to take a flying leap and forget about her. But that's me, Hard-Hearted Hannah."

Beth had seen Liz's point. Maybe the lack of sleep was making her paranoid. Maybe the calls had nothing to do with Nadia. "OK, I tell you what. I'll change my number. And then we'll see."

The peace that had followed immediately on the heels of the number change had been utter bliss. Beth had tucked under her cotton sheets each night, happy to be off to the land of dreams. But after only two weeks' respite . . .

"He called again!" she'd cried to Liz. "One A.M. This time the kid sang *Oh Beth, did you think you could get away so easy.*"

"But who'd you give the number to? Not Nadia!"

"I had to give it to the main office and to Agnes. But I was very clear that I didn't want it passed along to anyone else."

Agnes, of course, Beth had learned when she pressed her, had thought Beth had just forgotten to give it to Nadia. So when Nadia had asked . . .

Beth couldn't prove, of course, that Nadia had instigated the phone calls. All she could do was change her number a second time and share it with only Liz and Aunt Helen, hoping that neither Agnes nor any other of her school buddies would try to call.

Not that she'd seen much of the old gang outside of school anymore. Beth had joined the gang for pizza once in a blue moon but always found herself braced for Nadia's entrance, humiliatingly relieved if Nadia didn't show. She'd found it more and more difficult to fake pleasantries at the smaller lunches or the girls-only birthday parties with Nadia, the consummate actress, pretending to be as friendly as ever.

Nadia had been winning. Not that this was a game Beth had ever wanted to play. But by avoiding her school chums, hiding her phone number, she'd been ceding the field, allowing Nadia to push her ever further into isolation.

Beth, however, had other things on her plate. Every other weekend she'd driven to Elberton to be with Uncle Jack. And her creative writing class had been running her ragged, its core of super-gifted kids requiring that she up her game to meet their talents.

The school year's end had found Uncle Jack doing considerably better and her writing students reaping rewards. At the final faculty meeting, Agnes had announced that one of Beth's students had won first place in a state-wide poetry competition and another was having a story published in the *Kenyon Review*. Adult writers labored years to see themselves in print, collecting rejection slips, but this kid had made it first time out of the gate.

"Such a coup," Agnes had bragged. "Beth has brought us glory."

Beth ducked her head at the limelight but couldn't resist a glance toward Nadia, who gazed out the window as if she hadn't heard a word of it. Never mind, Beth had thought. The green respite of summer was within reach.

And what a lovely one it had been. Beth, Aunt Helen, and Uncle Jack had made a visit to the Sea Islands. Beth and Uncle Jack had gone trout fishing in north Georgia, and then to San Francisco. He'd fallen hard for the city when he'd shipped out of it in his navy days. Now it was Beth's turn.

"You ought to come out here and teach," he had said one afternoon as they strolled along the Sausalito harbor. "Not now, I know. But when I'm gone . . ."

She'd protested. He wasn't going anywhere. He'd shaken his head. "Yeah, I'm fine for now, but we both know how this story's going to end. And I want to rest easy, knowing you're happy. Something's been troubling you for a while now, and, best I can make out, it has something to do with your school. Sometimes it's just better to move on. In some instances a switch to something different is the best answer."

Beth had held that thought as September rolled around. Her classes had been promising again, with the exception of one section of wriggly freshman she'd taken on as a favor to Agnes. Nothing had changed on the Nadia front, but with Uncle Jack's health taking yet another downward turn as the fall moved toward the holidays, Beth had paid her little attention.

ONE GORGEOUS AFTERNOON LATE in the fall, Beth and Liz had gone shopping at the Sweet Auburn Farmers Market for quail and sweet potato cheesecake with which Beth was hoping to tempt Uncle Jack's failing appetite. The two friends had paused to listen to a gospel group's rendition of "Joshua Fit the Battle of Jericho" when around the corner came Nadia with two women, one older, one younger, both of whom bore a strong resemblance to Nadia.

Beth hadn't known what came over her, but she'd stepped right up with a hand extended, gleefully introducing herself and Liz to the two women, pretending not to notice Nadia's turning away.

The older woman had effused in the broad syrupy vowels of south Georgia, "How nice to finally meet one of Nancy's school friends. I'm Mary Brooks, her momma."

Nancy? And Mary, not Mimi? Oh my, Beth had thought. Then she'd laughed. "And I'm so pleased to meet you at last. Nadia speaks of you so often." She paused for a beat. "You know, you've done an amazing job of losing your accent."

"What accent?" asked the younger woman, who'd identified herself as Nadia's younger sister Lisa.

"Oh, I must have been mistaken," Beth had said, turning back to Mary Brooks. "Somehow I'd always thought that you were French."

"Darlin'," the woman had laughed, "I've lived my whole life down near Waycross, edge of the Okefenokee Swamp. The closest I ever got to France was some naughty lingerie the girls' daddy bought me one time. He's full of the devil, that old man."

Beth had been barely able to contain herself until Nadia and her family moved on, Nadia jerking them along for an urgent errand—imaginary, Beth had been sure. "She lied!" she'd exulted, hugging Liz, "Her family! Those stories about the Nazis! Nadia made it all up! She's not an only child! And, unless her mama's delusional, her daddy's not the least bit dead!" She paused. "Oh, my God. I bet her boyfriend Michael's imaginary too."

Liz had been stunned. "Jeez Louise, Beth. The woman's not only mean, she's crazier than a Bessie bug."

BETH HAD FOUND HERSELF dizzy with happiness, knowing that Nadia was a bald-faced liar. She finally had concrete proof that Nadia was not to be trusted.

She had still been reeling from the discovery when, a few days later, Hank tapped on her classroom door. "Got a minute?"

"Sure." Beth pushed back from her desk, wondering what this was about. She occasionally saw Hank around school or with the gang, but she couldn't remember his ever having stopped by her classroom before. She'd long since given up any romantic notions about him but wouldn't deny the little twinge she felt each time she heard he was dating this woman or that.

Hank had shuffled from foot to foot. "This is really weird. I don't know where to begin."

"Begin in the middle. That's what I tell my kids when they can't get started on a story."

"OK." Hank had perched on a corner of her desk. "So, this past Saturday afternoon, I'm playing a pick-up game of basketball, and there's this guy named Gene. We start talking. Turns out he's the Gene you dated for a while?"

"Yes." Beth had nodded, unsure of the question.

"Well, see, I was blown away, because I thought Gene was a woman. You know, J-E-A-N."

"What?"

"I heard the name mentioned, back, I guess, when y'all started dating, and, well . . ." Hank had smiled, grimaced, smiled again. "When you first came to Piedmont, I was dating someone. But then I met you, and . . . well, it took me forever to break off with her. It's a long story. By the time I got up the nerve to ask you out, a year had passed." He'd rolled his eyes at his own foot-dragging. "And I'd overheard something about your seeing somebody else. This Gene. Anyway I asked Nadia about him, and she said, 'No, no, J-E-A-N.' You were dating a woman, she said. That you, you know, played for the other team."

Beth had fallen back in her chair, stunned.

"I thought, well, you don't seem like a lesbian, but, hey, what do I know? And besides, if that's your thing, well . . ."

Beth had reached across her desk and laid a palm against his mouth. Then she'd laughed and wept all at once, her emotions a crazy kaleidoscope. Hank had wanted to ask her out, and Nadia literally queered the deal. What the hell else had she done?

"Well, I have something to tell you, Hank." By the time Beth had finished pouring out the history of Nadia's snubs, Nadia's lies, and her own pain, daylight had faded and she and Hank were sitting side by side in the dark.

He'd thrown an arm around her and drawn her close. "I have one more thing to tell you. Promise you won't scream?"

Beth had nodded, but she hadn't been sure.

"OK. You said no one in the gang noticed Nadia's being cold to you, but I did. I could see she was avoiding you, never laughed at your jokes. And then she'd do these little flurries of enthusiasm that seemed like they were just for show. So finally, one day when the two of us were alone, I asked her about it."

Beth had laughed bitterly. "I bet she said she didn't know what you were talking about."

"Not exactly. She said that you'd, you know, hit on her, and she'd turned you down, and so you'd gotten real nasty with her. That was why she avoided you."

Was there no end to it? "I hate her, Hank. I really truly do."

He'd enveloped her in a tight hug and kept hanging on. "Shhh, shhh. It's going to be all right," he had whispered. Then he had kissed her on the cheek. "Listen, now, I know you can't say anything to the others."

No. She'd tried that, hadn't she? Agnes had pretended concern, but Beth had seen that she really didn't want to hear it. For Agnes, peace in the department was paramount. And Big Bob, Santa Bob, whose broad shoulders she'd once tried to lay her burden on, had countered, "It's so sad when friends who are like sisters quarrel." There'd been no quarrel, she'd tried to explain, but he'd already chosen sides, and not hers.

"But it'll be different coming from me," Hank had continued. "I have no personal stake. At least, not one that they know of." He had ducked his chin, shy as a school boy. "You'll see. I promise, Nadia's toast."

Beth drove home in a happy fog. Someone else had known about Nadia after all. And not just someone, but Hank.

NEVERTHELESS, THE NEXT DAY, BETH found herself holding her breath as Nadia drew the first Secret Santa slip from the brown paper bag. Then there was Nadia shaking her head, grinning, and running a thumb and forefinger across her lips. Zipped.

When it was Beth's turn to reach into the bag, Hank caught her eye from across the office and winked. There now. It didn't matter if Nadia had stage-managed drawing her name again. Hank was on her side. He would spread the word. Soon everyone would know exactly what a liar, what a wicked person Nadia was.

Beth unfolded the small green slip. She'd drawn Nadia.

Oh, this was rich. What fun. Now, what should she give Nadia? A voodoo doll with a pin through its heart? A fudge cake with walnuts and Ex-Lax? How about arsenic? Even better, a handful of Uncle Jack's time-release morphine tablets crushed into the mix. *Do not crush or divide*, the label warned in large red letters. *To do so may cause potentially lethal overdose.*

The bell rang, ending morning break. On her way out the door Nadia greedily grabbed the last three brownies from the tin Beth had brought. Beth's mom's brownies.

"I hope she chokes," said Hank, close behind Beth as they exited the office. She laughed, and he squeezed her arm. "See you at lunch?"

Beth floated into her classroom. Fourth period, her star creative writing class. Today the young authors were to read aloud their latest efforts, the assignment having been to write a Christmas story. It was not, Beth had emphasized, to concern itself with sentimental clap trap. No accounts of the crippled child who gets his wish to visit Disneyland. No return of the prodigal daughter on Christmas Eve. Beth wanted them to challenge themselves, to rise above the usual, the expected, the trite Hallmark card thinking.

The class heard six stories, each better than the last. Then, her brightest light, a delightful girl named Melissa, prepared to read.

"Melissa," Beth said, "I suspect yours will be the last, all we'll have time for today."

Melissa took a deep breath and began. "Sharon had been nine, her last happy Christmas. At its approach, she grew dizzy with excitement. Santa, a.k.a. Mom and Dad, were going to give her, she just knew it, the bicycle she'd spied shopping with her mother one day at Lenox Square."

An electric shock sprinted up Beth's spine. The little hairs on her arms fried and frizzled. It was like some kind of flashback, a slip through a time warp. Surely she'd misheard. Melissa couldn't have written— "Pink and purple with confetti-like silver streamers hanging from the handlebars, it was the bike of Sharon's dreams. None of her friends in Ansley Park had anything anywhere near as wonderful."

Beth's breath grew shorter and shorter as Melissa's story continued, straight down the terrible trajectory of her own last happy Christmas. Beth's ears buzzed louder and louder, until she could no longer hear the words.

Nadia. Of course, Nadia. Melissa's drama teacher. Melissa was crazy about her, sang her praises often, as did other students, to Beth's great twisting pain. But Nadia had actually talked about her with her students?

Melissa finished reading and the room lay silent as the other students waited for direction. But Beth could barely breathe, much less speak. Finally Melissa herself asked, "Any comments?"

Then the bell sounded, and the students poured out the door. All gone except for Melissa, mouth atremble.

"Ms. McFarland," Melissa began, fighting against tears but quickly losing. "I'm so sorry. I know I shouldn't have, but I was so upset when I heard your story, and I couldn't get it out of my mind, and when I started writing . . ."

"That's all right," Beth whispered. "Really, Melissa, but where did you hear the story?"

"Ms. Brooks told us."

There. Nadia. But *us*. Plural?

"Last week we were doing scenes from *Medea* and having trouble with Medea's actions." Melissa's voice gathered strength as she went along, building her case. "You know, her desire for revenge against her husband that conflicts with her love for her children, who, y'know, she kills. Anyway, Ms. Brooks told us the story about your mom being killed."

If there was a connection between her own life and Medea's, it was lost to Beth, but perhaps that was because she was focused on other questions: Nadia told this story to an entire class? "My mom being killed?" Beth asked. "And what did she tell you about my dad?"

The girl bit her lip. "Well, that was awful, y'know, the part about his being left behind after your mom died in the Christmas Eve crash with her sister's husband beside her. Your uncle? Jack, is that right? He's still alive? Her lover?"

Beth, unable to stifle a moan, dropped her head in her hands.

"I'm so, so sorry, Ms. McFarland. I know I shouldn't have. It's just, when I started trying to write about Christmas, all I could think about was how I've felt so bad for you ever since Ms. Brooks told us about the crash. And then that other Christmas, in college, when your boyfriend left you for another woman and you took the overdose of sleeping pills . . ."

LATER, BETH DIDN'T REMEMBER what she'd said to Melissa, how she soothed her sufficiently to pry her from the classroom. She didn't remember lifting her dad's letter opener—long, silver, and sharp as a dagger (used mostly for opening book boxes)—from her desk drawer and slipping it into her skirt pocket. She didn't remember walking down the hall to Nadia's classroom. It was if she'd awakened from a nightmare, at a phone's shrill ringing, to find herself planted in a cold fury across from Nadia, who was eating lunch at her desk.

"You bitch. You miserable bitch."

Nadia considered her placidly, silently, for a long while. Finally she wiped a bit of egg salad from the corner of her mouth and answered, "Haven't you embarrassed yourself enough?"

"Embarrassed myself?" Beth took a single step closer, the weight of the letter opener pleasant against her thigh. "How have I done that?"

Nadia shook her head as if Beth were a willful child. "All this carrying on that you do. Look, I simply choose not to be your friend anymore. Why can't you accept that and go away quietly? Without all these never-ending histrionics?" Nadia bit into a pickle.

A step closer. "Ah," said Beth. "So you're singing a different tune. Up to now, you had no idea what I was talking about."

Nadia rolled her eyes. "This is really tiresome, you know." She polished off the last of her sandwich, then reached for a can of Diet Coke.

"Not tiresome for me." Beth's voice was icy, low, and controlled. "I find your hideous behavior fascinating, in fact. The phone calls you instigated. The lies. Telling people that I'm a lesbian, that I hit on you."

Nadia sighed heavily, dismissively. "You've really gone around the bend. But then you always get blue this time of year. This time, more than paranoid." With that, Nadia reached for the first of the three brownies, Beth's brownies, Beth's dead mother's secret-recipe brownies, resting on a napkin on her desk, and stuffed it into her mouth.

Beth's voice shook as it rose. "And the students? You lied about me to students. Told them my mother died in the company of her lover, my Uncle Jack? That I tried to kill myself? What the hell else have you conjured up in that sick brain of yours?" Within the depths of her pocket, Beth squeezed the handle of the letter opener, hard.

Nadia stuffed in another big chunk of chocolate, smiling, dark smears of fudge on her fingers.

Beth was in striking distance now. Close enough to see the pulse in Nadia's throat. She knew Nadia wouldn't think she had it in her, but she did.

Wouldn't bother me a bit, she assured herself.

But it would. It would bother her ferociously. Not the killing—she was poised for that—but the consequences: imprisonment, her life ruined. Nadia wasn't worth that.

Around a mouthful of thick cake, her consonants mushy, Nadia purred, smugly, "Will there be anything else?" Paused. Chewed. "Mmmm. Yummy."

Beth retreated a step, back towards sanity. "Trust me on this, Nadia, you're finished. And I'll never speak to you again."

Nadia chomped again, the second brownie gone, squinching her eyes with pleasure. "Promise?"

Beth nodded in the affirmative, even now delivering on that promise, her lips zipped. Then reached forward to pat Nadia on the arm, an ironic gesture of reassurance.

Nadia shrank back. "Don't touch me. Just go," she grunted, then stuffed the entire third and last brownie—Beth's thick, dense fudgy brownie made by loving hands at home—into her greedy mouth.

And choked.

FIVE MINUTES LATER BETH joined Hank in the English office for lunch. It doesn't take long, really, for a person to die when she's made a perfect pig of herself, clogging her air passage with food. Not that Beth had stayed for the very end.

What she had already seen before taking her leave was sufficiently unpleasant, particularly Nadia's beseeching eyes, the blue tinge of her face, the strange high-pitched wheeze of her labored breathing.

Nadia had slumped down, then fallen from her chair and onto the floor behind her desk. Beth had waited long enough to satisfy herself that Nadia would not revive sufficiently to reach the door or the phone in her room— not that she had been able speak or cry out from the moment the choking began. Beth, keeping her vow to neither speak to nor touch Nadia, had left the room.

Outside in the hall, hearing the door automatically lock behind her, Beth paused for one brief moment of panic. Fingerprints! But, no, not to worry. There would be no dusting of doorknobs, no scouring for clues, no

C.S.I. scurrying about. It was patently clear that Nadia had died by her own piggy fudge-streaked hand.

In the end, Beth had merely aped Nadia's example. She'd done nothing. Nothing at all.

"Hey!" Hank said as Beth entered the office, pulling out the empty chair next to him for her to sit down. Agnes was eating alongside Big Bob and Joanna and Tom and Charlie.

"We were just talking about you," said Big Bob. "Got any more of those fabulous brownies of yours tucked away?"

"Nary a one." Beth swiped her palms together once, twice, then three times for good luck—or to applaud a job well done. "But maybe if between now and Christmas, if you're very, very good . . ."

SARAH SHANKMAN is the author of seven novels in the acclaimed Sam(antha) Adams series of Southern comic-mysteries as well as the thriller *Impersonal Attractions*, the crime caper *I Still Miss My Man But My Aim Is Getting Better*, and the semi-autobiographical *Keeping Secrets*. Her short stories have appeared in more than a dozen anthologies. When not traveling, she lives in Berkeley, CA.

P.S. YOU'RE MINE

Michelle Richmond

W e were living in New York City then, in a small one-bedroom apartment on 84th Street, half a block from Central Park West. It was our fourth winter in the city, and we had already established our own Christmas tradition. We'd wake up around eight in the morning, walk to the Hungarian pastry shop on 111th Street, have hot chocolate and thick pastries, then walk back to our apartment to open presents. The meager gifts would be scattered beneath a two-foot tree purchased just days before from the Norwegian guys on the sidewalk outside Gristede's, one of those trees that comes already nailed to the wooden X. After opening presents, we would empty our stockings. My stocking always contained expensive lipstick and nail polish in outrageous colors, a candy bar, maybe an electric toothbrush or pair of socks. His always held a new CD by some British pop band, a box of malted milk balls, and a yo-yo or other toy I'd picked up at West Side Kids on

Christmas Eve. Each year, we both pretended to be surprised by the contents of our stockings, then devoured our candy and made love on the big living room rug in front of a space heater.

The pastries, the gifts, the exclamations of delight over the predictable contents of our stockings, even the lovemaking—all of these things were only a prelude to the real event of Christmas day. In the late morning we would walk through the quiet streets, our boots sinking into the snow, our breath quick and warm in the frozen air. Our destination was the movie theater at Lincoln Plaza. As we walked, I anticipated the hot, salty popcorn, the darkness and warmth of the crowded theater, the secret thrill of being a couple, quiet and complete unto ourselves, a pair of moviegoers among fellow moviegoers. To be this on a day when so many folks were enduring big family gatherings in small dismal towns made me feel very sophisticated. To have met this man, to have landed in New York City, to have avoided the inevitable discomfort of a family Christmas in Alabama—I was astonished by my own good luck. For a few hours I could almost forget the nagging conviction I'd had for the past few weeks. I could put out of mind the little details—the empty champagne bottle I found stashed in the trunk of my husband's car under a blanket covered with grass stains, the frequency with which he had begun to go into another room and shut the door when his cell phone rang, the increasingly lengthy business trips.

I thought of my mother's big house at the end of a cul-de-sac in Mobile, how the air conditioner would be cranked up high so she could roast marshmallows in the fireplace, how the wrapping would hardly come off the presents before she and my father started bickering. The night before, they would have gone to the enormous white church on the interstate to see the Christmas cantata and eat doughnuts in the fellowship hall. The night would have ended with a drive through the grounds of the mental hospital on the west side of town to see the living nativity. The drive would have reminded them of the son they had lost, my brother, who had hung himself from a light fixture at the age of seventeen, and the rest of the evening would be spent in silence. Every Christmas Eve for as long as I could remember, my family had gone to see the holiday display at the mental hospital, and even after my brother died there, my parents kept going, as if by adhering to tradition they might forget the unspeakable circumstances that tied us to that place.

We walked down Central Park West toward the theater. The taxis looked benign against the snowy backdrop of the park; they seemed to hover over the damp highway, their yellow shells glistening like spaceships. Snow did that to New York City; the silence and brightness of it made the city seem alien. On days when the snow was new, one had the feeling of being not in the city one had come to know but in a parallel version of the city, a slightly altered mirror image that existed in some other universe. That is why we continued to live there despite the crowds and the crime and the absurdly high cost of everything; living in New York was like living in many cities at once, and on any given day you never knew which city you would wake up in.

We turned left on Columbus, left on Broadway. By the time we reached Lincoln Plaza, our toes felt numb in our boots, and our faces were flushed from the cold. We purchased our tickets from the somber woman at the little window and stepped onto the outdoor escalator that would take us down to the theater. The joke about Lincoln Plaza Cinema was that you could wait until the movie came out on video and watch it on a bigger screen at home. Every showing sold out, and the theater seemed to draw the most aggressive moviegoers in the city, the type who would make you move two seats over so they could sit exactly in the middle, then fight you for the armrest. Still, I loved going there, maybe because it was where we had seen our first movie together in New York. Later we would discover the gorgeous Ziegfeld, the quirky Quad, the rowdy Sony on 84th, and the tasteful Paris; but Lincoln Plaza would always be special because we had gone there on our first night in the city. We'd seen an obscure Belgian movie, then stopped at Gray's Papaya on our way home. It was July, we were newlyweds, and the sidewalks were crowded with patio restaurants and dog walkers and girls in their summer dresses. We purchased two hot dogs and a papaya shake to share, and we stood at the counter to eat, watching the chaos of the street. Back at our building, we stumbled over boxes and suitcases to get to the only clear space in the whole apartment, the bed. The bed was crammed in next to the window, and we made love to the rattling hum of the window-unit air conditioner while condensation dripped onto the sheets. To this day, it is my fondest memory of New York.

Just ahead of us on the escalator, a petite woman with an expensive haircut and knee-high boots huddled in a woolen coat, clutching a small blue handbag. She was a sort of Manhattan everywoman, and I would have thought nothing of her had she not lifted her hand to tuck her hair behind her ear, revealing a tattoo on her right wrist. It wasn't a particularly artistic tattoo, and it wouldn't have been startling were it not for the fact that I had seen it before. The tattoo said P.S. The letters were about two inches high, in an elaborate script.

I nudged my husband. "I think I know that woman," I whispered.

"You think you know everybody," he said.

It was true. We rarely went anywhere that I didn't see someone who, at first glance, looked like one of my colleagues at the enormous public relations firm where I handled mid-level accounts. Usually, upon closer inspection, it turned out to be a stranger.

She turned her head, and I finally got a good look at her face. Yes, I did know her. Or had known her briefly, a long time ago. I felt a chill go all through me, remembering my brother. What on earth was this woman doing in New York? She certainly had cleaned up well.

"Stop staring," my husband said, but it was too late.

"Do I know you?" the woman asked, leveling her green eyes on me.

"Sorry." I fumbled with my scarf to hide my embarrassment. "You look very familiar."

"I get that a lot."

"You remind me of this woman—never mind. I'm sure it's a mistake." In truth I was sure it wasn't a mistake, but it wasn't the sort of thing one casually mentioned on the escalator. I recognized her from a religious youth rally I had attended in Alabama twenty years before. Back then, she was gaunt and aggressively sexy, decked out in tight red pants and hoop earrings. The theme of the event was "Salvation Lasts a Lifetime," and she had been the featured former prostitute—every Baptist youth rally has one—who had forsaken her lurid life on the streets for Christ. As one of the more zealous members of my church's youth group, I'd been rewarded with a backstage pass and had met her face to face on opening night, right after the pizza bash. When I shook her hand, I had noticed the strange tattoo and asked her what P.S. stood for. "My pimp forced me to get that tattoo," she said. "Just to remind me I could never get away from him. As in, P.S., you're mine, bitch." I was startled and thrilled by her language, ecstatic when she agreed to let me interview her for my church's newsletter. In truth, I had an ulterior motive. The interview took place the following day at the Tiny Diny, where over bacon and thick buttered biscuits I told her about my brother, his struggle with homosexuality.

"You've come up from the bottom," I said. "Maybe you could talk to him, tell him he doesn't have to be gay, that Jesus can save him from all that."

"Are you sure that's what you want?" she asked, her earrings bobbing with each movement of her head. "Sometimes it's best to leave well enough alone."

It shames me now to think of what I said to her, but I remember my words clearly. "How can you leave well enough alone when someone desperately needs help?"

We reached the bottom of the escalator and stepped off. We were forty-five minutes early for the movie, but the ticket holders' line had already begun to form along a red velvet rope. We filed in behind the woman, who was smiling now and seemed keen to continue our conversation.

"Want popcorn?" my husband asked. I wondered how he managed to maintain the day-to-day courtesy and affection, even as he deceived me. Was it merely a habit he couldn't break, or was it an attempt to make me believe everything was okay? Perhaps it was a genuine affection that he'd never lost, despite his new interests.

"Yes," I said, "and something sweet." I did not know how long I could play this game. For the time being, confronting him was out of the question. As soon as I brought up the empty champagne bottle, the secret phone calls, the increased frequency of his business trips, we would have to discuss the issue and come up with a solution. I would have to force him to choose; he would expect nothing less of me. Because I had no way of knowing how he would choose, I remained silent.

"And a Diet Coke?" he asked. I nodded.

I was glad to have him step away. We had met in our early thirties, and there was so much we didn't know about one another's pasts. "People don't change that much," he once said when I mentioned that I would like to have known him as a child. "As you grow older you get smarter, maybe fatter, you change your hair, possibly your politics, your taste in music, but your essential character remains the same." Maybe for most people that was true, but I felt no connection to the girl I had been at ten, or even fifteen. She was shy, overweight, and fanatical; I was outgoing, healthy, and devoid of religious conviction. I was more than a little ashamed of who I had been back then, ashamed of how sincerely convinced I had been that half the people I knew were going to hell. Ashamed of how easily I swallowed everything they fed me in youth group—all that stuff about how gays were perverted and Americans were the chosen people and my body belonged to God and my future husband. If he had known me back then, surely he wouldn't have liked me.

"Did you place me yet?" the woman asked, opening her purse and whisking out her lipstick case—a brown crocodile Chanel.

"Forget it," I said. "I was mistaken."

"Come on, say it." She seemed very amused by my discomfort. "What was I—drug addict? Prostitute? Cancer survivor?"

"I'm sorry, I—"

"Look," she said, uncapping a very red tube of lipstick. "Don't sweat it. This happens to me all the time. I'm a religious contractor." She held up a tiny mirror and applied the lipstick in two deft strokes.

"Pardon?"

"You know, religious contractor. I go to spiritual gatherings and talk about how my life has been changed by the power of the Almighty. Used to be I'd play a prostitute ninety percent of the time, but now that I'm older I more often get cast as a housewife who left her family to start a career but then saw the error of my ways. Helpmeet, that's a big word for me now. As in, 'I realized that God wants me to be a helpmeet to my husband.' The 700 Club is my biggest client—they're real into the wifely duties bit."

"I'm not sure I understand."

"Don't get me wrong, I'm not prejudiced in matters of faith. Christian, Jewish, Islamic, Wiccan, you name it, I've worked for them. The only group that doesn't seem to be in need of my services is the Buddhists, although I have attested on occasion to the spiritual ecstasies of tantric sex." She put the lipstick back in her purse. "Don't look so astonished, honey. It's a job, not a calling."

"So you never were a prostitute?"

"No," she sighed. "Not in the strictest sense of the word."

"What about the tattoo? P.S.?"

"My initials. I had it done in Cleveland about five years after I got into this line of work. It's supposed to remind me who I am. I had this story I used to tell about how I'd almost died in a crack house, how my pimp put a gun in my mouth and said I'd be worth more to him dead than alive. You tell any story enough times, you almost start to believe it."

"I remember that story," I said. "You told it at the youth rally— Alabama, 1985. You were very convincing."

She looked me up and down. "Let me guess. Baptist."

"How did you know?"

"With the Southerners, it's almost always Baptist." She took a small apple out of her purse and began to eat it, leaving waxy lipstick marks on the apple's green skin. "So, was I good?"

"What?"

"Was I good? Did you, like, get saved?"

"No," I blurted. "But my brother did." I couldn't believe I had told her that. Who was she, what right did she have to know? I glanced over to the refreshment stand and was relieved to see that my husband was waiting in a very long line.

"Good for him," she said, expertly tossing the apple core into a trash can several feet away. "I'm not particularly religious myself, but I do think faith has its advantages."

"My brother had been having some problems," I found myself saying. I couldn't seem to stop. "Drugs. Well, it wasn't drugs at first. He came out to my parents, and they really made life hard for him. Eventually they went so far as to have him committed. The drugs weren't the original symptom. They were just the consequence of coming out." I had moved closer to her and was talking very quietly. I didn't want anyone to overhear. In New York City at the beginning of the twenty-first century, my story sounded almost medieval.

"Same old, same old," she said. "If I had a dollar for every kid who pretended to find God because he thought it would save him from being gay." She opened her handbag again. This time, a bag of Tootsie Rolls came out. The purse seemed bottomless, like a magic trick or a cartoon. I imagined her pulling a bowling ball out of the purse, a pair of skis, a three-course dinner.

"So, the kid got saved," she said. "Good for him. Let me guess. He's married with two kids and serving as a deacon in his church."

"He's dead."

"Wow," she said. I could tell I'd really caught her off guard. She had been stiffly chewing a Tootsie Roll, and now her mouth stopped moving. She had no idea what to say.

"Salvation Lasts a Lifetime," I said.

"Hey," she said, regaining her composure, "if it gets you through the day."

"No, that was the theme of the youth rally, Salvation Lasts a Lifetime. You ended your speech with that line. I thought it was kind of weird, like the event planners hadn't really thought it through. Shouldn't it have been, 'Salvation Lasts an Eternity'?"

"I just read from a script," she said. "It's all the same to me. Look, I'm real sorry about your brother. I am."

"Thank you." Thank You. I must have said that a thousand times after my brother died. People would come up to me to express their condolences, and I'd say "thank you," as if they'd just given me a birthday present or complimented my hairdo.

My husband was at the front of the refreshment line now. He handed over his money, and the kid behind the counter passed him a bag of popcorn, a large drink, and a box of Whoppers. If he hadn't walked back to us at that moment, who knows what I might have confessed. Would I have reminded the woman about how she came home with me that afternoon after our interview at the Tiny Diny? Would I have confessed that we had ambushed my brother, forced our way into his bedroom, and demanded that he listen? Would I have reminded her how convincing she had been as she told him that if she could be saved from the streets, he could be saved from his sinful desires? Would I have described how they'd knelt on the carpet together and prayed? Would I have asked how it was that she could not remember?

Surely, I would not have rehashed everything. I would not have told her, or anyone, what I believed in hindsight to be true: if my brother had not been saved, he would still be alive.

My husband joined us in the line. He held out the bag of popcorn, and the woman and I, at a loss for words, both reached for it at the same time. Her fingers brushed against mine, and I pulled my hand back as if I had touched an electrical wire. "So," he said. "You're obviously old friends. Did you two figure out where you know each other from?"

I was fumbling around for an appropriate response when the woman chimed in, "We don't. I just have one of those familiar faces." The red velvet rope was unhooked and the line began to move. Inside the screening room, she hurried to the front, while we remained in back.

After the movie, I ran into her in the bathroom, and I asked, "Why didn't you tell him?"

"The past is the past."

"I appreciate it," I said, and then I felt dirty for saying it, as if by my gratitude I had somehow betrayed my brother.

"It's nothing," she said. "Merry Christmas."

On the walk home my husband asked if I'd like a hot dog from Gray's Papaya. "Of course," I said.

"And when we get home you'll call your parents," he said, a subtle command.

"Yes."

He was my conscience. He knew about my brother; he knew about my strained relationship with my parents back home in Alabama. But there were things he would never know about me, things that would always exist in another place and time. I wondered if he felt the same way about his affair—that it was separate from us, somehow irrelevant to our lives together.

I remembered one Christmas Eve, when I was ten years old and my brother was eight. I remembered how we got dressed up in red corduroy pants and green corduroy shirts that my mother had made, and the whole family piled into the car to go see the living nativity. My brother and I hunkered down in the back seat and stared out at Mary and Joseph, the wise men and the baby Jesus, all stationed just inside a plastic port-a-storage unit decorated as a stable. It was a warm evening, and we had the windows open. Our mother made our father stop the car so she could take a picture. Then, just as the flash went off, Joseph leapt toward the car and stuck his head in the window on my brother's side. "Boo!" he said. My brother shrieked in terror and scooted across the seat and into my arms. My father gunned the engine and drove away, but it was too late, my brother was already crying.

My mother turned around in her seat. "Don't worry, sweetheart," she said, in that voice she used to soothe us, to make us know we were safe. "They won't hurt you. They're just a bunch of lunatics." Years later, when I went to the hospital to claim my brother's body, that word would ring in my ears.

When we got to Gray's Papaya, the lights were off, and a gray line of snow had piled up along the bottom of the closed door. "Maybe the Krispy Kreme is open," my husband said, hooking his arm through mine.

"I'm not hungry anymore," I said. "Let's just go home." I was thinking of our small apartment, the built-in shelves piled high with books. I was baffled by the way gratitude and love and anger and jealousy could exist simultaneously, a delicate and explosive mix. I wanted to hit him, to tell him everything I knew and suspected, to make a big messy scene on the street. Instead I huddled closer to him. I was thinking of our tiny kitchen, how we would turn on the gas stove to heat the place up, how we would climb into our bed beneath the heavy quilts and sleep.

MICHELLE RICHMOND is the author of *The Girl in the Fall-Away Dress*, which received the Associated Writing Programs Award for Short Fiction, *Dream of the Blue Room*, and *Ocean Beach*, forthcoming from Bantam. She grew up in Mobile, Alabama, and moved around the country before settling in northern California. She currently teaches in the M. F. A. program in writing at California College of the Arts, and edits the online literary journal *Fiction Attic*.

A Singularly Unsuitable Word

Mary Anna Evans

I am so old that I remember when ladies didn't swear or drive automobiles. I recall a time when a young lady was considered fast if she let a boy hold her hand before he slid an engagement ring onto it. I'll be blunt. I remember Prohibition. How old do you reckon that makes me?

I remember my childhood, too, in a blurry kind of way. There were no hard edges in those days for little girls who were lucky, like me. There was no television to bring the world into my home, so I thought everybody had chickens and cows and vegetable gardens that gave them everything they needed to eat. I saw no reason why all children wouldn't have two or three toys to play with, just like I did. I was Florida-bred, so although I could well imagine that other folks might sweat occasionally—I certainly did—I had no notion of what it might mean to be cold. I went to Sunday School each week, so I knew there were bad things I shouldn't do. Still, for the first eight years of my life, those bad things were just numbers on the commandment list. What did killing and stealing and taking the Lord's name in vain have to do with me?

Perhaps my eight-year-old self was aware that I was infringing on one of those commandments when I filched a cookie shaped like a candy cane and crept out into that warm December night. Even now, I'm not sure which commandment covers spying on your sister, but one of them must. I knew I shouldn't be creeping around in my nightgown, following Iris, also in her nightgown, as she crept down the river path. I justified my actions by telling God (and Santa Claus, whose sleigh was probably on its way to my house right that minute) that if seventeen-year-old Iris couldn't manage to stay in the house when she was supposed to be asleep, then how could I?

I tried to be quiet as I skulked down the damp trail, but Florida riverbank foliage is lush and overgrown, even in wintertime. Iris should have been able to hear the spider lilies and palmettos rustle like crinolines as I pushed past them, but her mind was on something else. When she reached the landing, I saw what that something else was. Except it wasn't a something. It was a someone.

He was a man, older than Iris. He wore a driving cap pulled low over his eyes and a glen plaid vest so fashionable that it must have come from a city. Maybe Tallahassee. Pensacola, even.

I was glad to see that he was gentleman enough to take off his cap when he saw Iris coming. Then he tossed that fancy cap into the bottom of his flat-bottomed boat, stepped onto the landing, wrapped his arms around Iris, and commenced doing some ungentlemanly things. After a time, his behavior turned quite ungentlemanly—I'll refrain from discussing her behavior completely, if you don't mind—and there I sat, stuck in the palmettos until they got finished with whatever it was they were doing.

When another boat, a mighty big boat, arrived, they were in no condition to hear it coming, particularly since the two men piloting it came from upstream with their motor off, poling it silently into place beside the dock. With a careless motion, a thin, dark-haired man standing in front tied the heavily loaded boat to a cleat, surprising Iris and her ungentlemanly companion.

"And here I thought your deliveries was slow 'cause you was cheating me," said a second, burly man standing in back with his hand on the rudder. "Shit, Owen. You was just passing the time with this young slut."

The young man started to lunge toward him with both fists balled up but went dead still when the burly man pulled his gun. I swear, he stopped moving so fast that he was left standing on one foot with the other hanging in the air behind him. Iris, who had been busily arranging her nightgown, which was in quite some disarray, screamed. The sound stirred the hairs on the back of my neck.

"Come to think of it," the gunman said, "maybe I want to spend some time with the slut, too." His hand shot out and grabbed Iris by the waist. He hauled her into the boat, one-handed, without flipping the blamed thing, showing that he'd spent a lifetime on the water.

"Leave the girl alone, Gibson," his partner said. "This'll get us nothing but trouble."

"Shut up," Gibson said. "I'm done with the two of you." He waved the revolver back and forth between Owen and the other man, who I suddenly recognized. It was Mr. Robbins, who worked at the sawmill in town. "You're cheating me, the both of you."

"How can you say that?" Mr. Robbins asked. His eyes bugged out of his long sallow face every time the gun swung his way. "I go over the numbers with you every night. We count the bottles together before we deliver them. We count the money together when we get home. Then we pay Owen and we split the rest. When do we have an opportunity to cheat you?"

Gibson's eyes flicked away toward the woods for a second, and two things about those eyes scared me. First, they were unfocused, the way my grandfather's got when he'd had too much rum. And second, they showed a peculiar mix of confusion and humiliation, something I'd seen before.

My friend Jeremy, Daddy's field hand, had come home one day with that self-same look on his face. It was the day he got tricked into paying a whole dime for a little old candy bar because he didn't know his numbers. After that, I made it my business to walk to the store with him and look over the clerk's shoulder while he totted up Jeremy's receipt. Eight-year-old girls can get away with most anything when they smile, and everybody in town knew I'd been able to add a double column of numbers since I was six.

I'd been real proud of my tidy solution to Jeremy's problem, but on that night I felt as cold and rudderless as if I'd been dumped into the muddy river below me. I wrapped my arms around my knees and tried not to shiver. If my shaking set the spider lilies and palmettos to moving, then Gibson would know I was there. I didn't intend for him to point that gun at me, too.

He was going to shoot them—Owen and Mr. Robbins, and maybe Iris, too. That shamed, angry light in his eyes said that he saw no other choice. He needed the other men to help him run his business because he couldn't count the money, but he couldn't trust them not to cheat him because he couldn't count money.

Owen had eased his airborne foot down onto the landing, but his stance was odd and stiff, just like you'd expect of a man being held at gunpoint. Still, there was something funny about his right arm. He was holding it about a foot in front of him, with the palm pointed in toward his belly. Since I was situated where I could see that belly in profile, I was well-positioned to see something that Gibson couldn't—a bulge beneath that glen plaid vest. If Gibson was distracted, just for a moment, Owen might be able to save my sister, and himself, too.

I needed something to throw. A shoe would be perfect, but I wasn't wearing anything except my nightgown and underdrawers. I would have thrown them and sat there stark naked, but I couldn't imagine that they would make much noise.

Being as how Florida is nothing but a spit of sand, there were no handy rocks; but our swamps are full of cypress balls. I hefted one of them, a hard green knob about the size of a baseball, and heaved it into the river. It landed near Mr. Robbins's end of the boat, which turned out to be an altogether bad thing for him. Gibson hollered out a word I'd never heard before and pulled the trigger without a moment's thought, hitting Mr. Robbins square in the middle of his chest.

Poor Mr. Robbins toppled overboard and sank like a rock. Even though my sister was in the worst trouble imaginable and I wasn't in a much more secure position myself, there was a long heartbeat when all I could think about was Ginny Robbins, who was two grades ahead of me in school. She didn't deserve the news she was going to get come morning.

Now, let me tell you about the word Gibson said when he pulled the trigger, because it'll be important later on. In the years since then, I've heard that word several times. Not a lot, because people used to have some discretion about swearing in front of ladies. Certainly not lately, because you'd have to be some kind of a buffoon to swear in front of a doddering old woman like me. But now and then, someone has let it slip, so I've heard it and I know what it means, but I've only let it cross my lips once. I don't intend to do it again, so you'll have to figure it out for yourself. It rhymes with "love your truck." And it is a major violation of the commandment about honoring your mother.

At the instant Mr. Robbins lost his life, Owen went for his gun, but he took just a whisper too long to pull it clear of his waistband. Gibson's revolver went off again. Owen's shot went wild, and he pitched off the landing and into the river. Iris was making plenty of noise by this time.

Gibson smacked her a good one, started the boat's motor, slipped the boat from its mooring, and headed upstream with my sister. By the time they passed out of sight, I reckon I was making as much noise with my blubbering as Iris was with hers. It was only when I stopped to breathe that I heard the gurgling sound in the water.

IT IS A BLESSING that Owen was shot in the arm, because that left him two legs and one good arm to help me drag him out of the water. I might have been a smart little girl, but I wasn't as big as a minute.

He probably needed to sit there for a while and remember how to breathe, but there was no time. Gibson was hauling Iris upstream, but he had to navigate around a big oxbow and I knew a path that cut straight across the bend.

I grabbed Owen by his good arm and hustled him to the spot where we had a fighting chance to save my sister. He moved well for a man whose blood was dripping out and splashing on the ground. I knew that situation probably couldn't go on much longer, but we didn't have far to go. The path dead-ended at the river and, praise Jesus, we had gotten there fast enough.

The bank we stood on rose five feet above the river. We could have leaned over and spit on Gibson, but I paused for a second to come up with a more constructive way to use this strategic advantage. Owen might've ordinarily been a very smart man, but this wasn't his finest hour. He didn't stop to plan; he just launched himself, feet first, at a man who was holding a gun and had just proven himself capable of murder.

As I've said, the boat was fully loaded with cargo. The two men crashed so hard into one box that it busted open and let out a smell like the inside of my grandfather's flask. This time Gibson wasn't a good enough boatman to keep his vessel upright. Gibson, Owen, Iris—all three of them went into the river, and the fighting and cursing began in earnest.

I needed to help my sister, and I was going to need a distraction bigger than a cypress ball. I looked around. The riverbank sloped downward a few yards upstream until it was barely higher than the river itself, and the criminals in the boat below me had made good use of that fact. It was an ideal spot to unload boxes from a car directly into a boat, and the Model T Ford that they used to run their rum was still parked there, waiting for them. It was certainly bigger than a cypress ball, but I didn't have a clear idea how I could use it to save Iris and Owen. Yet.

As I ran for the car, I learned another curse word. It rhymes with "odd ma'am," and it is a serious transgression against the commandment about taking the Lord God's name in vain.

I must confess that the rescue plan I developed was at least as ill-considered as Owen's, but I was under duress. And remember, I was only eight years old.

It seemed to me that Owen and Iris were only a few feet from shore and that perhaps I could just drive the car out there and get them. The car would provide me some protection from Gibson's gun, assuming the revolver was even still dry enough to shoot. Once Owen and Iris were in the car, we could flee at top speed—thirty miles an hour, maybe more. It did not occur to me to wonder whether an internal combustion engine would work any better underwater than a revolver would. Cars were, in those days, new and magical beasts.

Like most children, I watched and memorized moves made by the adults around me. I knew how to advance the spark so the car would start. I knew I would find the crank on the floorboard in front of the passenger seat. I knew how to fit it into the housing on the car's front and turn it. I knew that I would need to pull it away fast when the engine started, so as not to have my arm jerked off. However, I did not—and still do not—know much about the braking system of the Model T. At some point in the process, I disengaged the brake and, when I knelt in front of the car, crank in hand, it started to roll.

Iris, God bless her, was in the middle of the worst night of her life when she looked up and saw a car driving over her cherished baby sister. To this day, I can hear her screaming, "Lila! Lila, look out!" I have rarely felt so loved.

She might have known that I had sense enough to lie down real flat on the ground between the wheels and let the thing roll right over me.

A runaway Model T splashing into a river makes a mighty fine distraction. Owen, who probably should have been more worried about me than he was, took the opportunity to wrestle Gibson into a headlock.

The sound of a baying dog and a man's steady voice reached me, and I knew my daddy had heard the gunshot and the screaming and had come to set things right. For all the years my father lived, I enjoyed the assurance that he would take care of Iris and me. That night was no different. Watched over by Daddy and his hunting rifle, his bird dog Sam, and Owen, Gibson was no trouble to any of us while we waited for the sheriff.

QUITE A CROWD HAD gathered on the river bank to gawk at Gibson by the time the sheriff arrived—news travels fast in places where nothing interesting ever happens—and a more somber group had gathered downstream to look for Mr. Robbins. The sheriff listened soberly as Owen told his story, shaking his head at his description of how Gibson had shot Mr. Robbins in cold blood.

Then Gibson raised his head and said, "The kid's lying. He shot Robbins, and then he tried to kill me. I shot him in self-defense."

I did not, at that time, fully realize the jeopardy that Owen was in. In those days before fancy forensic work, I doubt that anyone in central Florida could have told whether the bullet that killed Mr. Robbins had come from Owen's gun or Gibson's. Assuming their guns could be fished up off the river bottom, I imagine the lawmen could have told that they'd both been fired, but that's about all. This case would be decided based on eyewitness testimony, which, in my mind, wasn't going to be a problem. It wasn't a question of Owen's word against Gibson's. Iris and I had both seen what happened. Once we got the chance to tell our stories, I knew that everyone would see the truth.

I didn't understand that Gibson was a man of substance and wealth in our county, and the fact that his wealth was built on rumrunning didn't bother people all that much. Truth be told, a lot of the gawking onlookers were his customers. Maybe the sheriff was, too, for all I know.

I also didn't understand that the word of an eight-year-old child meant nothing then. Still doesn't, actually. And the testimony of a seventeen-year-old girl who had been caught visiting with her boyfriend in her nightgown could hardly have been taken seriously, not in those days. Women had only been granted the right to vote and sit on juries during my short lifetime, so our word might have been suspect to that crowd, even if we'd been upstanding citizens of legal age. I didn't understand these matters, but I sensed that things weren't going Owen's way, so I leapt into the breach. That has been my lifelong way of doing things.

"I saw him! I saw Gibson shoot Mr. Robbins right in the chest."

Women started murmuring about how a child hadn't ought to see such awful sights. They were right, but that was water under the bridge now.

"Why would he do such a thing?" the sheriff asked, getting down on one knee beside me. I could tell by his tone of voice that he was just humoring me. He had no intention of letting a little girl interfere with the august processes of the law.

"He thought Mr. Robbins and Owen were cheating him. Mr. Robbins explained to him that they weren't and I believed him. I think—" I hesitated to expose Gibson's ignorance, but he was a murderer and all, so I plunged ahead. "I think he can't read and do his numbers, and he was afraid they were taking advantage."

I saw a couple of people, including the sheriff, flick their eyes at the ground. Maybe I wasn't the only one who knew Gibson's secret. "Tell me exactly what happened," the sheriff said, so I did. I must have looked like an avenging cherub, standing there in a nightgown wet with riverwater and Owen's blood. I started at the beginning, and I told the story.

Perhaps I went into too much detail regarding the things Owen and Iris were doing at the landing because, for a time, every eye was fastened on my sister's mortified face. But when I described the two men floating downriver on a boat loaded with contraband, those eyes swiveled in my direction. When I delivered—word for word—the argument between Gibson, Mr. Robbins, and Owen, people listened. When I got to the part where Gibson shot Mr. Robbins, Mrs. Robbins moaned. Still, I had the sense that I was failing. None of these people would decide which man to put in jail based on the word of a skinny girl-child.

I imbued my description of the shooting with every lurid detail I could recall. The red spray of blood from the victim's chest. The smell of gunpowder and mud. The lonely splash of a body striking water. They were there with me, watching the murder. I could see it in their eyes. Yet they could not muster the faith they needed to act. I was still not a plausible witness.

Then I dropped the final fact onto my teetering pile of details, and they believed. I repeated the word Gibson had said when he pulled the trigger.

Everyone there knew me. They knew my mama and my daddy. They knew that no eight-year-old girl from a good family could possibly know that loathsome word. Some of the women in the crowd turned uncertain eyes on their husbands because they, themselves, had never heard it.

Later, when I told my story to the judge, I had been advised of how singularly unsuitable that word was for a young lady. Or an old lady or a gentleman of any age, for that matter. I refused to say it again, but the sheriff had heard my testimony the first time, and he explained things to the judge for me. Justice was served.

Owen did a little time for his rumrunning, but it was nothing compared to what he would have gotten for killing Mr. Robbins. I don't know if Gibson ever got out of prison. They may have hanged him, for all I know. That was not the kind of information that was shared with little girls in those long-ago times. Everyone concerned agreed that it was best to let Owen and Iris get married before he went off to jail. Just in case. She was waiting for him when he got home, and they lived together in a little house on the riverbank for the rest of their long lives.

Eventually, I stopped being a little girl and people started listening to me when I talked.

I take that back. After that night on the river, people paid heed to what I said, because I had proven myself. I believe some of them were a little afraid of me, which may have been why I came so near to being an old maid. Webster Simpson was the only man, other than my father, who could take me seriously without being afraid of me, so I married him. We lived next door to Iris and Owen for the rest of his long life, and we were happy.

Webster was a roofer by trade, but he was an artist at heart. There was nothing that man couldn't make with a piece of galvanized roofing and a pair of tin snips. He made Iris a tiny Model T, complete with tires that rolled and a tiny little crank on the passenger floorboard. She hung it on her Christmas tree every year until she died.

It's hanging near the tiptop of my own Christmas tree, right this minute.

MARY ANNA EVANS's professional background includes environmental consulting, university administration, and both technical and fiction writing. She is the author of *Relics*, the sequel to *Artifacts*, which won the Florida Historical Society's Florida Literature Award. It also received the Benjamin Franklin Award in Mystery/Suspense and was listed by the Voice of Youth Advocates as an Adult Mystery with Young Adult Appeal. Evans lives in Gainesville, Florida, with her husband, three children, at least eighteen musical instruments, and a cat. More information on her work is available at www.maryannaevans.com

MIRACLE BONES

Carolyn Haines

I tacked the last cedar-and-magnolia-leaf garland along the front porch balustrade of Dahlia House and stepped back to compare my garlands to those my mother had made during Christmases past. Mother had taught me well. I'd cut cedar limbs and magnolia branches from the backyard and tied them into long, looping ropes using gold tassels and red Christmas lights.

That's when I felt a chill at my back. No surprise; the weatherman had promised heaps of snow for Christmas Eve—a white Christmas—a true miracle for the Mississippi Delta.

"Sarah Booth Delaney, a white Christmas ain't worth a poot unless you got someone to snuggle with by the fire. Every good Christmas song is about a man!"

If I was tormented by Christmas past, I had good reason. I didn't have to turn around to realize Jitty, my resident haint, had come to torment me as the ghost of Christmas Present. "You're not going to spoil my good mood," I warned her.

"You been eating raw fruitcake batter?"

I turned to look at her and dropped my hammer. She wore the most fetching elf outfit I'd ever seen, on a ghost or anyone. The little green skirt, trimmed in red fur, barely covered what Aunt Loulane referred to as "possible." The dress had a tightly cinched red belt, offset by green stockings that emphasized her shapely legs. The plunging neckline, also trimmed in red fur, showed off Jitty's feminine assets to great advantage. If I hadn't dropped the hammer, I would have thrown it at her. Jitty never gained an ounce or aged a day.

"So, you've moved from the realm of ghost to elf. What a supernatural slut you are," I said wickedly.

"Someone has to help the fat man in the red suit."

"Go away. I was having a perfectly delightful time decorating before you arrived."

"You're just doing busy work to keep from thinkin' about that cold, empty bed."

"My bed is empty by choice."

"I suggest you revoke that decision and make a transatlantic call right now. Hamilton would be on you like a duck on a June bug, and that man can heat the sheets."

Hamilton Garrett V was a former beau. I was about to launch into a tirade about independence when Jitty held up her hand. "The phone's ringing."

I cocked my head to listen, and Jitty disappeared. The phone began to ring. I picked up the hammer and went into the house. My partner, Tinkie Bellcase Richmond, and I had finished our most recent private investigation case, and it wasn't likely that someone would be calling to hire us on Christmas Eve, but I hurried to answer it anyway.

Cece Dee Falcon's desperate voice rattled me. "Sarah Booth, you've got to help me."

Cece, who'd been born Cecil but decided to opt for femininity, was seldom desperate, especially not when she held the power of society editor of the *Zinnia Dispatch's* holiday section. Those she excluded never recovered socially.

"What's up, Cece?"

"Sarah Booth, I've done a terrible thing."

This raised my eyebrows. Cece wasn't one to beat up on herself, even when she might deserve it. "What happened?"

"You know the nativity scene at the corner of Main and Holcomb?"

"Sure." It was a Zinnia tradition that went back at least a hundred years. In a place where the past is dying a hard death, folks tend to cling to tradition. I'd driven by it just the night before and admired the fortitude of the young people standing motionless in the cold. The farm animals had not been as fortitudinous or cooperative, and Mr. Brown's donkey, which had been fitted out as a camel, had kicked one of the wise men who got too close. The wise man had been rushed to the hospital, disrupting the peacefulness of the nativity scene for a bit but suffering no serious injuries.

Cece continued. "You know the plastic Jesus?"

"Yes." They always used a plastic doll for the baby in the manger. One year they used one that could wet its diaper. The doll had a leak and froze to the manger. When the girl playing Mary tried to pick it up, it exploded. Call me anti-Christmas, but that is still one of my favorite holiday memories.

There was a long pause on Cece's end. "Well, the baby wasn't plastic, not this year. At least not for my photo."

I looked out the window at my Christmas garland and had a bad feeling. "What do you mean *not this year?*"

"I needed a picture for the society page. And I needed a real baby in the photograph."

"And—"

"I borrowed my cousin Miranda's baby son, Christoph. She and Roscoe went off to Memphis to do some last-minute shopping, and I agreed to babysit Christoph for the day. I did, after all, need a Jesus." Her voice hitched a little higher. "But then I got to fiddling with my camera, and next thing I knew I was back at the newspaper office—"

"You forgot Miranda's baby in the manger?"

"About four hours ago. When I went back to get him, he was gone."

"Cece!" I could be careless, but this took the cake. Cece may have had a surgical gender change, but the doctor had failed to install a single shred of the maternal gene.

"I'm not used to tending a baby. I can't believe it, either. I just forgot until I spotted his diaper bag in my office. Then I rushed right out to retrieve him, but he was gone."

"What about the other people in the nativity scene? The kids. Maybe one of their mothers took him."

"I've already called. They're just kids, and they weren't paying attention to a baby." Her voice broke and she sobbed. "What am I going to do?"

"We'll find him." I didn't remark how lucky she was that she hadn't found the little infant frozen blue. "I'll call Tinkie and get her on the case."

"What am I going to tell Miranda?" she asked.

That was an area where I didn't have any expertise—explaining to a mother how I'd lost her baby. "Let's don't tell her anything until we start the hunt."

"Good idea."

After she hung up, I called Tinkie, my partner in crime-solving.

"How could Cece *forget* a baby?" Tinkie's greatest dream was to have a child, but she had yet to convince her husband, Oscar, to share that dream. I, on the other hand, understood Cece's lapse of memory. Despite Jitty's constant nagging at me to produce an heir to haunt, I wasn't interested in babies.

"Cece was working. She got caught up in her story."

"Enough to leave an infant in thirty-degree weather?"

"It was an oversight." How had I ended up defending Cece?

"If anything has happened to that baby, she'll be charged with a crime."

"If anything has happened to that baby, no one will have to charge her with anything because the guilt will kill her."

Tinkie considered this. "You're right. Let's find little Christoph and make everyone's Christmas merry."

"I have a plan," I said. "I'll meet you at the nativity scene."

"What's the plan?"

"Sweetie Pie's a hound. She can track down the babynapper."

"Perfect." Tinkie hung up.

We arrived at the scene simultaneously. Sweetie jumped out of my roadster and rushed to Tinkie's Caddy, hoping to see Tinkie's miniature Yorkie, Chablis. Her wish was granted. The little fluff ball leapt to the ground and shook her salon-glitzed hair.

"I brought back-up," Tinkie said.

We walked the dogs to the currently empty nativity scene. I directed Sweetie over to sniff the manger, to put her on the baby's scent. Almost immediately, she and Chablis took off down Main Street. I could hear Tinkie's stilettos—she was too fashion-conscious to wear sensible boots—skidding on the icy sidewalk behind me as we gave chase to the dogs.

Sweetie and Chablis disappeared around the corner. When I caught up I found them, tails wagging, at the entrance to the First National Bank. Sweetie pawed the door, whining. When Tinkie arrived a few seconds later, out of breath and limping in her heels, she looked at me. "The bank has *been* closed. It's Christmas Eve."

I didn't have a retort, but I did bend over and pick up a tiny blue bootie that had fallen into the bushes.

COLEMAN PETERS, THE SHERIFF of Sunflower County (and my permanent heartthrob), stood at his desk and listened to Cece's tearful side of the story. Coleman already held a report that told the basic facts— Christoph Becker, six-month-old son of Miranda and Roscoe Becker of Issaquena County, was missing. Coleman didn't feel the need to tell Cece that the Beckers were one of the most prominent families in the state (given that Miranda was her cousin), and that once Roscoe realized she'd misplaced his son, Cece was going to be toast.

"The baby's been missing—"

"Four and a half hours." Cece hung her head in misery.

"At least you didn't find him frozen in the manger. I'm sure somebody picked him up and took him to the hospital or some other care facility. I'll get Gordon to check there for you." Coleman put his arm around Cece. "Sarah Booth and Tinkie are going to pursue the bank angle. We need to find out if anyone went into the bank today. Oscar will know."

Tinkie nodded. Her husband, Oscar, was president of the bank. "Oscar went to the golf course at the club this morning." She pulled out her cell phone and punched the numbers. "If you can believe that. Golf on Christmas Eve. And in this weather. Here's his voice mail. Oscar, call me immediately." She hung up and dialed the club's golf pro, who informed her that Oscar had never made it to the club that morning.

"Now there's something else that's missing," Tinkie huffed.

Coleman looked at Cece. "Go back to the nativity scene and wait. Maybe whoever took the baby will see you and realize you're looking for him."

Cece nodded as she rose.

"We'll find Christoph," I told her. "He's just fine."

Cece blinked away tears and was giving everyone a hug as her cell phone rang. She snatched it out of her purse and answered. Her face paled. "Hello, Miranda." She listened for a long moment. "No, that's no problem." She dropped the phone into her purse and looked at me. "Miranda and Roscoe had car trouble in Memphis. They're renting a car and will be here around midnight."

Tinkie guided her out the door. "We'll have that baby back and in your arms before dusk."

We stepped outside, and I glanced at the sky. The thick, heavy gray clouds seemed to hang no more than twenty feet off the ground. The first delicate flakes of snow began to fall as Cece drove away.

"All of my life I've wanted it to snow on Christmas Eve." Tinkie shivered. "Now all I can think about is that poor, freezing baby." At least at this point I didn't have to worry about Tinkie's frostbitten stiletto-clad tootsies. I'd unearthed a pair of fur-lined boots from her Caddy, and with the aid of threats, she had put them on.

We went back to the car where we'd left the dogs. Chablis's little paws were clicking against the window, and a large circle of frost had formed where she'd barked and barked. I opened to door to see what was the matter. To my horror, Sweetie Pie was gone.

"How did she get out?" Tinkie asked.

I shook my head. "I don't know. I guess she learned to open a car door." A set of dog prints in the frost-covered grass showed us that Sweetie had run back in the direction of town.

WE DROVE AROUND FOR ten minutes without finding Sweetie. Little Chablis leaned on her front paws on the dash, searching as hard as Tinkie and I.

"We have to give up," I said. "Sweetie can find her way home, but I guarantee you Christoph can't."

Tinkie nodded. "The snow is really sticking."

That was not the miracle I'd been praying for, but she was right. An inch and a half of snow had already settled over everything. The entire landscape of the Delta changed into a winter wonderland with that coating of white. And it was still coming down.

"Oscar hasn't called back. That worries me." She tried several numbers on her cell phone, all without result. "I told him not to go out this morning, but he hasn't missed a Christmas Eve golf match with Daddy since before we married."

"Oscar is a grown man, Tinkie. He's fine."

"If he isn't, he has no one to blame but himself." She tightened her scarf. "Let's go by the bank again."

We'd just made another sweep of the bank when my cell phone rang.

"Hello."

"Sarah Booth! I had a wreck. County Road 14. I found a—" The rest was garbled static, but I recognized desperation in Oscar's tone. I checked the number and saw that it was his cell phone.

Tinkie stared at me. "You look white as a ghost."

"That was Oscar. He's in some kind of trouble—"

"He certainly is. He told me this morning before he left to play golf that he was sick of Christmas and will be glad when it's over. He's such a Grinch. He said miracles were made up to soothe the masses, to 'keep the ignorant and superstitious in line.'"

Oscar and Tinkie had been going through a rough patch, but I'd always figured Oscar for smarter than that. Tinkie was the most joyous person I knew, especially when it came to Christmas. Miracles were an everyday fact for her. When Oscar dissed miracles, he was dissing Tinkie.

"Maybe he just woke up on the wrong side of the bed."

"Maybe." She gazed out the window as she absently stroked the whining Chablis. "Ignore him for now. If he's in real trouble, he'll call back."

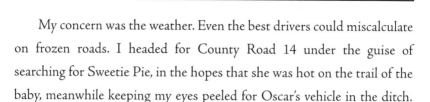

My concern was the weather. Even the best drivers could miscalculate on frozen roads. I headed for County Road 14 under the guise of searching for Sweetie Pie, in the hopes that she was hot on the trail of the baby, meanwhile keeping my eyes peeled for Oscar's vehicle in the ditch. Now we were hunting a husband, a baby, and a hound.

We cruised down Main, passing the empty nativity scene. Cece paced in the snow in front of it. Soon the town would bustle with those who came for their annual visit to the living nativity and Santa Claus, whose giant sleigh had been set up one block down.

We left the town behind us and drove in white silence. Tinkie tried to call Coleman and then Cece, but her cell wasn't working. The snow was falling thicker and thicker, and our time was running out. We were several miles out of town when the road began to disappear.

"Look!" Cece pointed. "Is that Sweetie?"

Sure enough, loping down the road was my runaway hound. It was hard to see in the falling snow, but it seemed as if she disappeared into a small copse of trees.

"Let's get out and follow her." Tinkie started to open the car door, without waiting for me to stop. I pulled off on what I hoped was the side of the road. It was impossible to tell. Snow had covered everything. I'd lost all sense of direction. Zinnia was somewhere behind us, but for all purposes Tinkie and I were lost.

"If we get too far from the car, we'll get lost ourselves."

"Chablis will lead us." Tinkie snapped a rhinestone-studded leash on the little moppet. Chablis promptly sank muzzle-deep into the snow.

"Tink, this is a bad idea."

"Nonsense. Let's get that dog and get back on the search for Christoph."

Not one word about Oscar, though. I sighed and followed her into the whiteout. It was better to be with Tinkie than remain alone in the car.

Chablis plowed valiantly through the snow. Tinkie, whose faux leopard-print coat was discernable in the snow, kept moving forward, and I followed. We made it to the trees, and a snow-covered branch whacked me in the head.

In the distance I saw something red. The snow was falling so thickly that I couldn't be certain, but Chablis whined as a dark figure jumped from a snowbank on the right. Sweetie! She circled my legs once, then dashed ahead. Chablis strained against her leash, trying to follow.

"Tinkie!" I called, my voice muffled by the snow.

She was peering forward, through the falling white. "That's Oscar's car!"

Whatever she'd held against him was gone. She ran through the snow, Chablis bouncing after her. Sweetie was already there.

Oscar's car was smashed into a tree. I could make him out, slumped against the steering wheel. I tried my cell phone to call for an ambulance, but there was no signal.

Tinkie pulled the door open, and Oscar tilted out and down into the snow. From inside the car came the wail of a baby.

Tinkie lifted Oscar onto her lap as she sat in the snow. I felt his neck and, to my relief, his pulse was strong. Snow began to collect on his forehead, and Sweetie licked his face.

His eyelids fluttered open, and he looked up at Tinkie's concerned face. "The baby," he said.

The infant was on the floorboard of the front seat. One bare foot waved in the air, and he cried louder as soon as he saw me. I'm sure he was cold and hungry and very unhappy.

"Oscar, where did you get the baby?" Tinkie asked as she helped him sit up.

"Someone left him in the manger on Main Street. I was going to take him to Sheriff Coleman, and then I thought—" He wiped his forehead. "I thought maybe we could keep him."

The bump on his head was obviously more severe than it appeared. Oscar wanted no children; he'd told Tinkie so numerous times. Besides, babies didn't stray, like dogs.

I held the baby in my arms, rocking him gently and snuggling him under my coat. I saw Oscar's cell phone in the snow and picked it up. To my surprise, it had a strong signal. I dialed 911 for an ambulance.

"These cell phones, so unreliable." I handed Oscar his phone. "When you tried to call me earlier—"

"I didn't call you," he said. He tried to gain his feet with Tinkie's help but gave up the struggle and sank back into the snow.

"Yes, you did. You said you'd had an accident on County Road 14. That's why we're out here."

He frowned. "I didn't call you. And this isn't County Road 14. It's the road to Hilltop."

It wasn't my nature to argue with a man who'd just survived a wreck, but I couldn't help myself. "Oscar, you called me. I didn't hallucinate the call."

He looked around at the clearing. The snow had stopped as suddenly as it started and a weak sun broke through the layer of cloud. "I don't know how you found me, but I didn't call anyone."

Even dizzy, Oscar was as stubborn as ever. In the distance I heard the sound of the rescue ambulance arriving.

Tinkie held Oscar's head in her lap. "Can we keep the baby?" he asked before slipping into unconsciousness.

TINKIE HELD CHRISTOPH AS we sat outside the emergency room, waiting for Cece to arrive. She blew in the door with a big smile and long stride, and in five seconds she had baby Christoph in her arms.

"Thank you both," she said, kissing the baby and then us. "Thank you. This is the best Christmas present I've ever gotten."

"You should thank Oscar." I tickled the baby's bare toes. "He found Christoph. He even wanted to keep him."

Cece held the baby out and examined him with a critical eye. "He is a fine baby, but to want to keep him . . . I just don't see it."

Meanwhile, I was still puzzling over Oscar's phone call, Sweetie's getting out of the car, the incredibly deep snow that still blanketed the ground, the very fact that Oscar had stopped and looked in the manger. There were a lot of factors out of whack. I listed them to Cece and Tinkie. "And what was Oscar doing on County Road 14? Where was he going? He was lost."

We sat in silence for a long time. "It's a miracle," Tinkie said at last. "This is the season for miracles, and each of us got one. Cece got the baby back. I got my marriage back. And Sarah Booth got her hound back."

Miracles indeed, I thought as I looked out the hospital window and saw Sweetie Pie and Chablis frolicking in the snow.

A native of Lucedale Mississippi, CAROLYN HAINES has written numerous works of fiction, including a series of mysteries set in the Mississippi Delta, the latest of which is *Bones to Pick*, due in early 2006 from Kensington. Her latest novel is *Judas Burning*, also available from River City, and a crime novel, *Penumbra*, is coming soon from St. Martin's Press. She worked for ten years as a journalist in the 1970s and currently resides near Mobile, Alabama, where she teaches fiction writing at the University of South Alabama. She is a past recipient of an Alabama State Arts Council writing fellowship.

SWIMMING WITHOUT ANNETTE

Alix Strauss

The guy in the blue scrubs slides Annette out from the wall. The sound is jarring, like the clanking of loose silverware in a kitchen drawer. The thick, white sheet that covers her body is removed. From my angle, it looks as if someone has smeared eye shadow all over her neck.

"I reckon he came up behind her and grabbed her like this," the medical examiner says, reenacting the scene. He inserts his hand under her. I hear his fingernails scrape against the metal slab as he scoops up her head and wraps his hand around her throat, placing his fingers over the large bruises. I take a picture with Annette's camera. He looks up at me, startled by the flash.

"You know, I could lose my job."

I smile at him, the way my mother taught me during a time when she still had high hopes of my being with men, and rest my hand over his. "You have really nice hands," I say. His face eases. I stroke his index finger and his ego at the same time. "So soft," I add.

He smiles and pulls away, leaving me holding Annette's neck up by myself. My fingers just touch the bruises, my hand too small.

"Anyway, you can't tell anyone you've taken these." He suddenly looks like a young boy, his body thin and shrunken. The light blue medical uniform seems out of place against the steel-colored room. I remove my hand, place Annette's head gently on the table, focus the camera, and shoot. The clicking and fast-forwarding sounds reverberate off the sterile walls. Everything feels hollow and heavy at the same time.

I want to bend down and kiss Annette, stroke her hair, run my thumb back and forth over her forehead above her eye, like I did when she'd have a headache from working in the darkroom too long. Even dead, she looks beautiful, her pale skin like a half-baked apple pie. Her body is cold and stiff, her eyes fixed upwards. I close them, my hand brushing over her face. My fingers touch her dry lips, caress her cheek. The bruises, bright blue, brown, and yellow, almost glow off her body. I lean my ear down towards her mouth as if I expect her to say something. To whisper his name. Say mine. Utter the word *love*.

I identified her body three days ago. I was flying back from New York. Some of the shirts I design were being photographed for *Elle*. Annette was supposed to join me, but a work conflict kept her in Atlanta. Instead, I watched a movie starring Meryl Streep by myself, her seat unoccupied on the plane, my hand kept company by stale pretzels and a bitter Bloody Mary. I called the apartment when I landed at Hartsfield, then tried to reach her on her cell. I wasn't alarmed until I saw the squad car perched in front of our awning. Even then, I thought they were waiting for someone else. On the way to the coroner's I kept thinking, how would Meryl handle this? She's always so controlled.

Annette's face was dirty and bloody, her clothing damp. I wanted to lift her off the table and take her home. Soak her in a hot bath with scented green-apple soap, dress her in my favorite flannel pajamas. I would have brought her back, warm and clean.

The police wouldn't allow me to stand closer than six feet. The medical examiner hadn't arrived yet, and everything was considered evidence. I pleaded with them to let me bring her a change of clothing. Crumpled to the floor and begged. They picked me up, walked me out, and put me in a car. One of the rookies drove me home, the siren off. I sat in the back seat and watched the handcuffs that hung from the gate swing back and forth, knocking against the window.

"We better go," the examiner says.

I nod and take a few more photos. I think about developing them myself. Annette taught me how, but I haven't been able to go into the darkroom yet. Instead, I deliver the film to a one-hour photo place near the university. I tell them I'm taking a forensics class and that the photos are a bit gruesome, then ask, "Do you give student discounts?"

THE POUNDING OF HOUSE music from the nightclub above is light enough to be annoying, but not loud enough for me to make out the song. There's an uneasy hum; the clicking of cups against saucers, an occasional stir of a spoon against ceramic, the sound of the waitress's croaking voice asking if I want a refill, all seem distorted. The diner takes on a ghostly feel, as if waiting for something to happen. As if time has slowed down. Even the air seems to move cautiously.

I glance at the clock above the register—10:05 P.M. For the past six hours, I've been waiting for my lover's killer. I have decided to look for him on odd days of the week: Mondays, Wednesdays, and Fridays.

Annette was here a month ago. Sitting in this spot, perhaps, her camera bag and equipment on one side of the padded booth, grant and fellowship applications on the other. It was outside this restaurant where he grabbed her, threw her down, his hands ripping at her neck, his fingers pressed into her skin, nails cutting her flesh. It was in this alley where her body lay sprawled on the cold pavement. Blood mixed with loose negatives, rolls of undeveloped film, lipstick and wallet tossed like shells on the beach. I visualize the approach, see him needing help of some sort, maybe asking for directions or claiming he was sick. I picture him with thick, dark hair and sharp features. He's tall and broad, with clear skin and charming good looks.

Annette and I met at a friend's Halloween party in Macon five years ago. Twenty of us were shuttled out to an old inn minutes from the Rose Hill cemetery where the event was taking place. I stood behind her, waiting for room assignments. She had the most beautiful lips, soft and full, like feathers or white daisies. Her eyes were magnificent, iridescent, and her hair had a silky, ash-colored glow. I remember wanting to slide my hand over to hers and see what her skin felt like. Wanted to stand close enough to smell her perfume.

That night, we sat in the parlor with the other guests, drank chardonnay, and inhaled cheese puffs with artichoke mousse dip. The night was sticky and balmy, dinner rich and heavy. Later we kissed outside on the back porch. She'd put her arms around my back, brought my hips close to her, and for one moment, a brief second you can't grab on to, I was whole and immortal. Almost nothing.

The door opens. The humid air rushes into the diner, catching me off guard. A man walks in with another woman. Her arm is hooked through his, and they laugh as if they've just come from a ritzy cocktail party and are sharing an inside joke. They take a seat off to my left. He's tall, broad, and terribly attractive in a Gatsby sort of way. He's wearing a dark green trench coat. I write all this in my notebook.

I sit here and wait.

I drink my coffee. I watch others. I think of a plan.

THE FIRST VICTIM WAS a married gynecologist who'd bought three pairs of shoes from the store next to the diner. They found her several hours later in the stairwell of her apartment building, a patent leather flat crammed into her mouth, her neck broken. The second and third were club kids from the after-hours lounge a few blocks from here. A matchbook from the diner was tucked into the cellophane wrapper of the Marlboro package in one of their pockets. They were spotted on the street, arms linked together, bodies flopped over like Raggedy Ann dolls. People assumed they were homeless kids who'd passed out on the street after a night of partying. In their laps was loose change from well-meaning strangers. The fourth lived across the street. She had just brought dinner from here. I imagine the food still hot, the fries greasy, bun getting soggy, cheese on the hamburger turning hard as she struggled to open her door. Maybe he came up behind her and offered to help. Maybe he said he was visiting someone and she let him in. Police found her body propped up against the wall, aluminum foil take-out container opened and placed purposely in her lap.

The prints they pulled from the victims are useless. There are no hair follicles, no clothing fibers, no skin embedded under any of the women's fingernails. Still, the cops have assured me they're doing all they can. They have round-the-clock surveillance, detectives in unmarked cars positioned outside, an undercover cop dressed as a homeless person in the alley where Annette was found. They look at me funny, eyes shifting away from me when they tell me this, their impatience elevating each time they see me at the station. They are no longer interested in my write-ups or my photos of restaurant patrons. At first they took them with interest. Now they sit in a folder at the bottom of a pile of manila envelopes on someone's desk.

The pungent odor of unwashed hair and sweat floats by. It belongs to the biker boy who wears a thick chain and combination lock around his neck. It clinks as he walks past me. One leg of his nylon workout pants is scrunched up at his knee; the other hangs down over his sneaker. Gold rings decorate most of his grimy fingers. It's time to go.

AT HOME, WITHOUT ANNETTE, I look for a place to sit. A place where my body will fit comfortably into the crevices of emptiness. There are traces of Annette everywhere, tangible evidence that prove I once lived with someone: Special K cereal, a camera bag, her photographs. The light, dizzying smell of her burns through the walls, like cooking aromas from the neighbor next door. I've had the rugs cleaned and repainted the apartment; still she hangs in the air.

Photos of her body are spread out everywhere, along with the police file and autopsy report, making my apartment look like a detective's office. I've collected a mass of folders, too. Lists of specialists, orthopedists, criminologists, and therapists, along with printouts from Internet sites dealing with murderers, profiler gurus, and unsolved FBI cases, are stacked in neat piles on the floor. The wall next to the dining room is decorated with her as well. I've replaced Annette's beautiful photographs with large bulletin boards. They display fingerprints, hand charts, and the photos I took at the morgue. When I can't sleep, I stare at them. I resurrect her voice, recreate her laugh, place a mental picture of her in the antique chair we bought together at Sweeties flea market, and ask her to tell me what happened.

I think of her smile as I run my hand over the one of the blown-up photos of her face. I place the tip of my index finger over one of the bruises and trace the outline of her neck. This is the part of her I miss most. The way she'd toss her head back when she'd laugh, her ash hair spilling over her shoulders, over her eyes. She'd take her fingers and run them just above her scalp and pull the hair away from her face. I inch my thumb over her lips, aching to feel them on my mouth. I miss her teeth. The light clicking of enamel when we'd kiss, sucking her lower lip, the feel of her tongue. When she worked late, and I was already in bed, she'd slide in next to me, smelling of silver chloride and fix bath, place her lips just over my earlobe, and say, *I'm home.* We'd lie in bed, our bodies intertwined, our voices just above a whisper, while the glow from the TV illuminated the room.

A HEAVYSET WOMAN THUDS into a booth; I catch her reflection in the window. The double chin makes her look deformed. Her face is tense, her eyes glassy. She looks as if she's going to cry. The staff calls her Lindsay.

"Need a menu tonight?" the waitress asks, placing a Rolling Rock in front of her. Her arms are so large that her watchband digs into her wrist. It looks as if the thin leather strap will snap at any moment. I wonder what kind of mark it leaves at night, if she takes it off, if she lets the suffocating skin breathe. I wonder if he's watching her and if she will be next. Maybe it's me who's caught his eye. Maybe it's my name on his list.

Knowing he might be here is all I have. It's the only thing I can hold on to. The only thing I can do to help. So I wait and watch and listen and stare and observe.

I came here every day in the beginning. Dragged Annette's parents and my brother here, too. All three humored me. We sat for hours, nursed bad coffee, ate tuna melts, and picked at fries.

AROUND THE SECOND WEEK of October, the waitress asks if I've gotten a job nearby since she's noticed me eating at the diner so often. I nod yes, surprised it's taken her this long to ask.

"What do you do?" she inquires, setting silverware in front of me. She's dressed in a black-and-white waitress uniform. Her name tag reads Doris.

"I'm a clothing designer. I make T-shirts."

"Oh," she exclaims, her face opening up like a flower bulb. "How exciting."

I smile politely and pull at my sweatshirt, trying to remember what I'm wearing underneath. Something I've made, or did I merely throw on a white T from the Gap? Sometimes I wear whatever I've slept in.

Annette and I had our first date a week after we met. She showed up with expensive wine in a pretty bottle, its true color hidden by its protector, and a Christmas ornament, a star made of thick, frosted glass. While she opened the wine, I twirled the star in my palm by its tall top spire and nearly pierced the skin there. I joked that I would have to find a tree with a thick top, just to support the weight of it.

Our conversation poured from our lips and became an extension of us, a sexual desire to share information. Annette, a lightweight, got tipsy on her second glass and passed out on my couch. I sat with her head in my lap as one of my hands ran through her hair, my other resting on her arm. I inched my finger underneath her spandex sleeve, felt the softness of her skin, the firmness of her muscle. The smell of her perfume was so calming to me that I sat there for hours listening to her breathe. Before she left, she kissed the star, leaving a perfectly imprinted lipstick mark on it.

"To a new year of bliss and happiness," she said, her lips moving from the star to mine.

I refused to wash it and placed it on the console for all to see. It became a running gag when she moved in three months later.

"Would you wash this thing already?" she'd say, handing it to me when we'd do spring or fall cleaning.

"You're soooo sentimental," I'd coo, taking it from her grasp and replacing it in its rightful spot. "It's all I have to remind me of our first date."

"I'm living with you. How much more of a reminder do you need?"

When friends came over, it was always mentioned, especially at holiday time, when the body of our Christmas tree would be dressed in red and white flickering lights, but its top still bare.

"Karen's made me immortal," Annette would joke with inquisitive guests, holding up the object for all to see. "I'm a bona fide rock star. She won't even let me put it on the tree. She thinks I'll break it." Everyone would laugh, and I'd blush and sip wine quietly on our couch.

The last time someone mentioned it, Annette teased that I was planning to auction off her photos and the star on eBay. "Maybe I should sweat on something or drool on a napkin? Perhaps I should just go around the apartment kissing things?" Then she waltzed over and kissed me, leaving the shape of puckered lips printed on my cheek. I feel this spot now, longing for her lipstick mark to be there.

At the table next to me is a professor from the university, working on a laptop. He's balding and wears wire-rimmed glasses and bites his thumbnail in deep thought. I call him the Nibbler.

I've categorized all the men, defining them by a code system Annette would appreciate. Trench Coat Man isn't well. I've watched the way his hand shakes when he lifts a cup of coffee, and I wonder if he has Parkinson's. I cross his name off my mental list. Bad Hairpiece Man doesn't seem to have the stamina or the personality for killing someone. He became hysterical last week when a roach crawled over his spoon and under the table. Biker Boy is still a suspect, and so is one of the waiters who lost his temper last Friday over a small tip left by a group of teens. I look around for new people. I look for Annette, half expecting her to bounce through the diner door and yell *surprise*.

I VISIT NEIMAN'S AT Lenox Square. They're having a pre-Thanksgiving Day sale on men's gloves. I test myself to see how good I've gotten at measuring size. I ask the saleswoman to take out several different pairs. She lays them out on the glass counter. I finger the soft leather, asking, "Eight and a half?" She looks inside and nods. I go down the line like a game show contestant or circus act, each time giving the correct size. The last pair is a 9 1/2, an inch bigger than the killer's. I try them on, want to see how my hand takes up the space inside. They're warm and soft, and my fingers feel lost in them. I walk around aimlessly, looking for Annette, listening to Christmas Muzak sung by dead crooners. Bing Crosby, Judy Garland, Elvis, all insist this was a wonderful life.

On Monday, I interview an orthopedist who specializes in hands. "He's tall, six-two, six-three," he says. His voice is crisp, and he keeps looking at his watch instead of at the crime scene photos. "You can tell because of the angle and the position of the bruises." His phone rings, but he's kind enough to ignore it. "He's probably a righty. He pressed harder on this side of her neck. See?"

Next, I go to a palm reader, a proclaimed psychic, and show her the same pictures. I lay them out like Tarot cards.

"This man is angry. Very angry." She looks up at me, waiting for a reaction. When I don't say anything, she continues. "He is filled with rage." She drops the photos as if looking at them is channeling too much pain for her. "You should stay away from him," she advises as she sticks my twenty in the pocket of her flowered housecoat.

THE DINER IS UNUSUALLY crowded, packed with high-school kids in sports uniforms. Their varsity jackets and scarves are clumped in seats. I scan the restaurant, see the regulars, make a few mental notes. The Nibbler is typing away in the back. Pinhead, a man whose head is smaller than the rest of his body is off to the side, eating with a woman who looks like a hooker. The Hamburgler is here, too. He only orders hamburgers smothered in mayo and drinks three or four beers with each meal. I don't see Biker Boy or Mustache Man. A thin, sickly looking guy is eating chicken pot pie in the corner. I've had my eye on him for some time, and he acknowledges my presence with a nod and a half grin. I return the gesture while eyeing his dry, blond hair; his lips are thin and red, like those of a girl. I spot an empty stool by the counter next to an attractive woman who's smoking and playing with the end of a salad.

Normally I sit in the back, which enables me to see most of the diner. Other times I take to the front where I can watch people pass by outside and still see customers inside. At the counter, my back is to most of the patrons. There's a long mirror across from me offering a panoramic view, but teas and cereals are stacked on the shelf, cutting into my sight. Plus a large refrigerator that houses the desserts—generic cheesecake, chocolate cake, apple pie, green Jell-O, and a bowl of fruit with Saran Wrap past its clinging stage—intersects the left side of the restaurant.

"Tuna on whole wheat?" Catrina asks, already scribbling something down. The waitstaff knows me by now. I almost look forward to seeing them.

"I think I'm going to break out of character and order a ham-and-cheese omelet."

Catrina nods, erases what she's written, and starts over. She tears off the slip, sticks it on the ordering thing, and yells to the chef in restaurant short-talk.

"That's always a safe bet," says the woman sitting next to me. She smiles and tilts her head to one side.

My stomach hurts, and I'm not sure I'm in the mood for conversation.

"Hope," she adds, blowing smoke out of the right side of her mouth.

"For what? Not getting food poisoning?"

She's pretty. Reddish hair, soft green eyes, and full lips painted a tawny brown. She looks about thirty-eight, maybe a few years older than me. I study her face for a second. She scrunches up her nose and narrows her eyes in a playful way as she flicks her cigarette and leans into me.

"No, my name is Hope."

"Your parents must have been very optimistic."

We laugh and stare at each other. I'm about to look away when she reaches for my face. "You have something, an eyelash," and brushes her index finger an inch or so under my eye.

No one's touched me like this since Annette's funeral, and it feels as if I'm watching a movie, as if my skin isn't real. She moves back to her original position.

"What's dinner without a little wine?" She raises her empty cooler bottle by the neck and wiggles it like she's ringing a bell. Catrina nods. "And one for my friend." Then back to me, "I always feel better having a partner in crime."

"It's been a long time since someone bought me a drink," I say, fidgeting with my napkin.

"Well, I'd be more than happy to buy you another when you're ready."

Hope rubs her index finger around the edge of the glass a few times, seductively, like I remember my mother's friends doing at dinner parties. It makes a high-pitched sound and I wonder if she's flirting with me. Annette had terrific gaydar. For a lesbian, I seem to have been overlooked in this department.

"I'm Karen." I eye Hope's Ultra Light cigarettes, suddenly longing for something to occupy my hand. "Which is a stupid name. It sounds like I'm a carry-on-bag."

She giggles and tosses her head back, just like Annette would do. Then I remember why I'm here.

Catrina sets my food down. The well-done omelet, the golden brown french fries prepared just as I requested all make me nauseous. I take one bite, feel full, and start to cry. Hope leans in closer to me and strokes my hair.

"Can I do anything?" Her voice is as soft as a cashmere sweater.

I shake my head no and, in an effort to stop the tears, look up toward, the door. I see Bad Toupee Man walk in. I click back into professional mode and take out my notebook.

TODAY, I'M SITTING AT the table closest to the register. Taped to the wall are glossy school portraits and some pictures of children sitting on other children's laps. A calendar displays the month of December with a picture of snow-covered mountains. Fake mini-trees with tiny plastic presents glued to them reside on each of the Formica tables. They're a new addition, an attempt to make the place festive. Three elderly ladies sit gabbing to my right. I can smell their perfume, heavy and too sweet, their voices as shaky as their hands. They talk about their grandchildren, their pets, their lonely lives. Men in overcoats sip coffee, their jackets still on, cell phones resting on the tables.

The diner is uncomfortably quiet, and I haven't seen Hope in three weeks. A small hole has been created since our evening together. It feels as if she, too, has disappeared. I've thought about calling. We exchanged numbers, and the paper sits folded on my nightstand.

Trench Coat Man is here again, sitting beside me. So is the Hamburgler. Lindsay slouches off to the left, face buried in the paper, her fat hands clutching the uneven ends. I asked if she wanted to sit with me, but she said no, her voice so soft I could barely hear her.

I've started conversations with strangers. Invited myself to join single men for lunch or dinner. Inched my body into the seat next to them, claiming the restaurant is too crowded or that I work at home alone and that the presence of another person is so important even if we don't talk, which we eventually do, because everyone in Atlanta is lonely and sad and needs to speak to someone. Anyone who will listen. And I do. I become all eyes and ears. I learn their stories. I pry without looking as if I am. It's not hard. People are eager to share. I stare at their hands as they rest on the table or hold a fork, grasp a plastic glass, each time mentally measuring them. Then I go home and compare my hands to the life-size posters in the apartment.

LAST WEEK I FINALLY spoke to the Hamburgler, whose real name is Lincoln.

"As in log?" I had joked with him, his fingers gooey with mayo. We were sitting a few stools away from each other. He flashed me a toothy grin.

Tonight we make polite chitchat. He's a construction worker in the city. So are his two brothers, but none of them works for the same company. His father's a retired cop; his mother's a social worker. He owns a jeep. He's cute, tall and broad, but has too much gel in his hair. Most impressive are his arms. They're toned and muscular like the beer poster where the guy's shirtless and is holding a cat in one hand, a Bud Light in the other, a red bandanna around his neck.

"Anyway, that's my deal." He wipes his mouth with a wet napkin and stands up. "It was good talking to you." I watch as he tosses a few dollars on the table and walks slowly up to the register.

I wonder how tall he is.

"See ya," he says.

"See ya," I echo.

He pays the bill and sticks the remaining cash into the back pocket of his jeans.

"WHERE YOU GOING?" LINCOLN calls when I walk outside. I watch him flick his half-smoked cigarette to the ground. It lies there lit and smoldering.

"Home." I'm dazed from the thick air of the diner and almost get knocked over by people hurrying home, anxious to get out of the cold snap's freezing mist, their collars turned up against their ears, faces hidden by scarves. Their arms are laden down with shopping bags filled with elaborately decorated Christmas gifts, and their thoughts are of parties and family dinners.

"Where's that?" Lincoln asks.

I tell him, and he offers to walk me there. My mind races. I strain to picture his hands. "Sure." I try to think of something else to say. "Let me guess. You're just a good old Southern boy trying to be neighborly?"

He laughs. A warm, rich laugh, like a game show host, and for a moment I think, I must be wrong. No one with a laugh like that could kill anyone. I'm disappointed and confused, but we keep walking, his stride equal with mine even though my legs are shorter.

"Daddy told me never let a lady walk by herself at night. It ain't right." He smiles and shrugs, shy and sly at the same time.

Despite the cold, I start sweating and perspiration drips down my back, the kind my mother complained about during her menopausal years.

We reach my corner. The diner is only a few blocks away, but it feels as though we've been walking for most of the night.

"So." He clasps his hands together. "It's still kind of early. Want to get a drink? See the tree? Aren't they lighting it tonight?"

I try to picture what Annette and I would be doing right now. Christmas was her favorite. She'd buy too many presents, insist on making eggnog from scratch, leave the tree up past New Year's, 'til it was anorexic-looking and pine needles carpeted our floor.

"Okay." I search his face looking for clues. His eyes seem kind. He has nice ears. "I'd like to change first. You want to come up for a sec?" I finger Annette's metal X-Acto knife in my pocket, the one she used to cut negatives with.

He lifts his eyebrows and leans his body forward, rocking onto his toes, hands shoved into his coat, which is open so I can see the worn logo on his Braves sweatshirt.

We're quiet in the elevator; neither of us has anything to say until we get to my floor.

"Nice building. You own?"

I can't tell if he's staring at me or past my head, like the police do when they want me to leave and have more important matters to take care of.

"Yeah. I've lived here for eight years." I unlock the door; the snap of the metal cylinder reverberates in my hallway. The smell of beer on his breath and hamburger on his clothing is enough to make me gag. I wonder what I'm doing as I hit the lights and walk in.

Like an expectant mother who's packed a suitcase and placed it in the hall closet waiting for the exact moment it will be needed, I, too, am prepared. I've hidden a tape recorder in each room set to voice activation. The police reports, files, and journals reside on the top shelf of my closet. The photos have been stripped from the walls and Annette's work put back to its original spot; black-and-whites from our trip to Vietnam, a photo that appeared in the *Chronicle*, the series of tombstones she did from our Rose Hill Cemetery trip, which won her a Guggenheim, hang on the wall with pride.

"Do you want to take off your jacket?" I ask, hanging mine up in the hall closet. I feel him come up behind me. A hand slides over my waist and around my stomach. His breath on my neck feels locked in my hair. I place my hand over his and, like a blind person, search for a size. I feel as if I've spent my whole life waiting for this moment. He squeezes my ass lightly with his free hand and playfully brings his body closer to mine.

"You smell so good," he whispers, his lips just touching the skin under my ear.

I lead him into the living room. More mirrors. Better angles.

He leans forward and kisses my lips harshly, knocking me momentarily off balance. My hip collides with the edge of the dining room table.

"Sorry. You okay?" He looks concerned. Maybe I'm wrong. I should stop this now.

"Fine." My hand reaches for the bruised spot, but his hand gets there first. He rubs at my hip in small circles. Then he bends his head down toward my neck and starts to kiss me. With each kiss he backs me up closer and closer to the wall. I want to move. I want to push him away, tell him this is a mistake. That I've made a mistake.

His lips are at my ear when he utters, "What are you thinking?"

"How nice you feel." I can stop this now. Ask him to leave. Tell him the truth. Anything.

"Really?" He smiles and grabs at my arm, clamping it against the wall up near my ear.

"Let's take a breather," I suggest, my mind racing.

"Why?" His voice is even-toned, like a golf announcer, void of any feelings; he leans into my pelvis.

I think of the last time I was in this position. Annette had pinned me up against the wall in our hallway, spread my arms up above my head like a policeman frisking a criminal, and kissed me on my neck, my ear, my arms.

Lincoln's whole body rests on me, causing the knife in my pocket to dig into my skin. I try to maneuver my hand down to adjust it but he's got his leg pressed into my crotch. He leans in harder, one hand still holding down my arm, his other moving up to my throat, right under my chin.

Lincoln lifts up my jaw, like a chiropractor working on a patient, his thumb and index finger at each ear. I feel my vertebrae elongate, and a slight pulling starts at the base of my spine. I see his forearm, make out the edge of his watch. I flash to Lindsay's fat arm, think about how hard a time he'd have holding her down. As big as his hands are, they might not fit around her neck.

I try to smile and look as if I'm enjoying this. "I like it rough." My voice is hoarse. I move my free hand to his thigh for a second, then inch back toward my own pocket.

"Do you, now?" he whispers.

I feel a wet spot on my leg, feel the blood staining my pants from the open knife, and wonder if he'll notice.

Above my head is a photo of Annette and myself. It's a small picture set in a silver frame. We were at Chastain Park before a show, and a friend snapped the photo. I stretch my hand up, thinking that if I can cause the picture to fall he'll have to move, but his grip is too strong. My fingers reach, but feel nothing. I see his eyes glance up and over my head. He looks from the photo to me. A smirk forms on his lips, and his eyes are like slits.

"She's pretty. Your sister?"

"Girlfriend."

His smile widens.

My body is shaking. A numbed, prickly sensation comes over me as I envision Annette fighting for her life, trying to scream or hit him with her camera.

"Ever done it with a man?" he asks.

I want to swallow. It's hard with his fingers around my throat. My free hand searches for something, anything. "Have you?" I croak.

He pulls at my sweater, bringing me to him, then shoves me harshly back into the wall. My head snaps back. My eyes try to focus. I become aware of several things: my jerky movements, my breathing, the smell of hamburger. I look around the apartment in quick bytes to see what I can grab on to for protection. The crystal vase on the dining room table, too far away; the phone wire to twist around his neck, too complicated, too many movements. I reach out on the wall, feeling around on the bar for a bottle of gin or vodka to whack him on the head with, or the wine opener to jab him in the eye. My hand comes up empty, then feels something cool and sharp.

I grasp whatever it is and smack it against the wall. He turns away from me to look at what I've found. I'm holding a heavy, jagged piece of glass in my hand. He moves toward me and without thinking, I stab downwards. He backs away screaming, an earsplitting shrill. Then he lunges, trying to grab at my chest. I drop to the floor and find another shard from the star, this one with Annette's lipstick imprint, still intact. He surges at me, and I shove the glass into him, and slide away as he falls, his head ramming into the coffee table on his way down.

His body hits the floor.

All is quiet.

I kick him in the head. Watch a mat of black hair sweep my floor.

No movement.

My foot juts out and I strike him again, same spot. Still nothing. I turn him over. I think he's breathing, or maybe the breathing is mine. I can't tell. Pieces of Annette's Christmas ornament are sticking out of his neck. His eyes are bulging. Blood oozes out, staining the Indian rug. I bend down, place my hands around his neck. My fingers searching for the exact position. Like hands on the keys of a piano after endless hours of forced practice, as if they remember, each creating their own private musical sound, they grip tighter and tighter as he gasps for air. I feel his pulsating veins, see his protruding eyes get bigger. Blood seeps out of the puncture on the side of his throat. Glass digs into my skin. I pull back. My hands are thick with blood, as if I've been finger painting. I slink back to the wall, lean up against it for balance. Then I notice something, the light reflecting off the large piece of glass still stuck in his neck. Annette's smudge-proof lipstick insignia, a trace of bright red. And from my angle, it looks as if she's kissed him.

ALIX STRAUSS has been a featured lifestyle trend writer on national morning and talk shows on ABC, CBS, CNN, and VH1. Her articles have appeared in the *New York Times*, the *Daily News*, *Time Magazine*, and *Self*, among others. "Swimming Without Annette" is taken from her collection of shorts, *The Joy of Funerals* (St. Martin's Press.) Strauss's work has been anthologized, and her short fiction has appeared in the *Hampton Shorts Literary Journal*, *Quality Women's Fiction*, and *Stories from the Blue Moon Café III*. Her short story "Shrinking Away" won the David Dornstein Creative Writing Award. She is the recipient of several awards and fellowships, including the Wesleyan Writers Conference and Squaw Valley's Screenwriters' Summer Program.

Yes, Ginny

Suzanne Hudson

Ginny Widdamacher's stepdaddy, Johnny Lee Fowler, went missing sometime Christmas Day, though no one could be sure when. After all, there were friends and relatives in and out, gift-wrapped boxes blotting out some of the routine family scenes, ripped paper tearing holes in the underlying goings-on of the place and its blurred boundaries. A spirited din of raucous voices drowned out what secretive, soul-seducing sounds might be heard in the ramshackle mobile home were it not a holiday.

Johnny Lee's absence was first mentioned around midafternoon, and the family was hard-pressed to remember when, exactly, they had last noticed him, passed out in his perpetually worn purple-and-gold plaid pajamas. As always, the LSU cap was turned sidewards on his head in a way that annoyed Ginny's mama no end. Everyone agreed that he had spent at least some of Christmas day there in the La-Z-Boy recliner like the lump that he was, deaf and numb from the Old

Charter. Ginny's relatives, a collective noun of arms and legs and faces, whose conversations writhed in and around one another's like muscled reptilian snarls in a pit of stranded snakes, offered theory after theory about where Johnny Lee Fowler had got off to. He went to the A&P to buy cigarettes and watch folks come in for batteries for their bawling kids' toys. He went to the bowling alley that never closed, to drink with Pete and Bootie and Killer Jones, derelicts all, and who were all surely there, as they were every other day of the year, listening to Johnny Cash on the jukebox and swapping lies. He went to harass and romance Connie Babb, that skank of an ex-girlfriend of his, the one he went to prison over, for slicing her across the cheekbone with a switchblade knife. He went outside to take a leak and passed out in the woods. He went somewhere, anywhere, driving his muffler-loud Chevy, with a belly full of booze and an attitude, and got himself locked up. Again.

But Ginny, six years old and swept up in the magic of Christmas, didn't care where Johnny Lee Fowler was or where he might be. She didn't like him. He was mean to her mama and mean to her brothers and mean to her. He sat in her real daddy's burnt orange recliner and yelled to be waited on by her mama, bossed her brothers to do their chores, and squint-watched her for the least little mistake so he could call her a doofus or a retard or a maggot head. And when he got up from that chair, he staggered and stumbled and shoved and slapped and punched. Sometimes he fell out in the floor, and the family would step over him as if he were not there, mouth gapped open, drooling saliva, a cigarette's dying glow clamped between his hairy knuckles. So Ginny was nothing but glad of the fact that he had disappeared.

She spent the day rearranging the cardboard furniture in her Barbie Dream House, making up pretend dramas with Barbie and Ken and Skipper: Skipper running away from home and becoming a trapeze artist; Barbie kissing Ken because he saved her from a thing kind of like the Blob;

Barbie throwing furniture at Ken because he liked Skipper better than her. In between conjured-up dramas, she played languid games of Candy Land and Chutes and Ladders with her older brothers; bent the wrists and joints of her brothers' G.I. Joe dolls; and pretended to be a majorette in the uniform Santa Claus had brought her, ignoring the frayed places along the hem. The relatives spent the day cooking and talking and laughing and bickering and cursing and drinking and only later in the day wondering just where the hell Johnny Lee Fowler had got to.

"That's a stupid damn thing," Johnny Lee had said to her, early that morning when the light was dim, his hangover thick, as she ran her little-girl-smooth palm over the Dream House, awed and proud. "Ain't nothing but a cardboard box. And somebody's hand-me-down, too."

She didn't answer back. She never did. She already knew that the Santa who visited her got his toys from the fire department. The fire department had a used-toy drive every fall, toys they painted and repaired for the poor kids, the nondiscriminating children they thought wouldn't notice a nick here or a ding there or a scratch underneath. Last year, Ginny took one of her Santa presents, a Tiny Tears doll, to show-and-tell in kindergarten, and another little girl, Glendaline Moorer, came up to her afterward and said, "That's my old doll I gave to the firemen. That right there's where I stuck pushpins in her leg." And she pointed to a scattering of bore holes in the pricked, pink plastic flesh. Ginny just pulled the doll's dress down over the leg, as best she could.

Johnny Lee Fowler had moved in last summer, loving on her mama, pretending to like Ginny and her brothers, doing little odd jobs around the trailer, calling their home a tin can, and calling himself a stepdaddy. He worked at the paper mill until summer, when he claimed he hurt his back, then badgered Ginny's mama into quitting her job at the Ben Franklin and going to work at the mill herself, working the night shift, making better money, enough to barely pay the bills, but still not enough to draw the Santa who delivered brand-new toys. That Santa visited the other side of the creek, where Glendaline Moorer lived, where the little girls wore shiny hair ribbons and pressed pinafores with white eyelet ruffles.

For his part, Johnny Lee collected a government check, every cent of which went to the liquor store in town or for Alpine cigarettes or for bets on games of pool, or, as her mother accused from time to time, for other women. He planted himself in the recliner and looked at the TV when he wasn't out with his buddies. He ensconced himself in that chair for hours on end, thumping cigarette ashes into the honey-colored glass receptacle on the TV tray at his right side, reaching for the bottle of amber liquid on the floor at his left, anchored to the spot by the whiskey and the fuzzy glow from the television screen. "Turn that damn hat around," her mama would say to him. But Johnny Lee just sneered, "Can't see the TV good enough with the bill out front," and the only time he turned his hat frontwards was when he made to leave the house. Ginny loved to see his hat turned frontwards.

Ginny and her brothers were allowed to sit in the living room with Johnny Lee in the evenings but were not allowed to pick any programs and had to watch whatever Johnny Lee Fowler wanted to watch—*The Ed Sullivan Show, Alfred Hitchcock Presents, Perry Mason, The Twilight Zone*—until he ordered them to bed. They knew not to argue, knew not to dispute or resist or offer up any evidence that they had anything like thoughts and feelings of their own.

Ginny shared a tiny room beside the bathroom with two of her four brothers, sleeping wedged against their calves and heels at the foot of the bed. Whenever she couldn't sleep, she listened to the night, to her brothers' snores, to the television until it signed off with the crescendoing strains of "The Star-Spangled Banner" and turned into hissing gray snow, to the uneven steps of Johnny Lee's bare soles against the linoleum as he stumbled for the bathroom. She listened to the wall groan as he leaned his palm against its opposite side while he used the toilet, trickling his imprint into those spaces in the little trailer where her own wishes and dreams resided, and she began to wish on him, on his intrusion. She began to wish him away and into thin air, like that magician did the lady in the box on Ed Sullivan's show; she wished him broken down on the stand, like Perry Mason always did the bad guys; she wished him into a suspense-filled fantasy, into the twilight zone of no logical explanation. And all that wishing, it seemed, had all of a sudden paid off, because now, on Christmas Day, he had vanished.

As the afternoon dimmed, the relatives began to fret and froth and rail about that sorry Johnny Lee Fowler and his nerve to skip out on the family on such a day, to rise up out of his drunken wallow to go and do something else, something he deemed more important than the day Jesus was born. They demanded answers of his empty chair. What about the children? Wasn't this their day? Didn't he realize how disappointed the little ones were? But, most of all, wouldn't he catch it when he got back home! And they offered Ginny's mama advice about how to adequately punish Johnny Lee for his holiday season sins. They rolled their eyes and ate more turkey and drank more beer and vodka and gin and whiskey, while Ginny and her brothers played in their walled-off worlds of pretend, the living room a sprawl of toys and dime store candies and nuts and apples, the hot-bulbed lights on the four-foot-tall tree burning her brothers' skin whenever they wrestled each other into its branches, the children apart from the relatives and apart from one another beneath their intersecting play.

Sashaying around the room in her majorette uniform, Ginny would every once in a while, out of the corner of her eye, catch the pattern of Johnny Lee's purple-and-gold pajamas, or see the sideways-turned LSU cap that made her mama so mad, and feel a small shudder at the nape of her neck. She would cut her eyes to the place where his presence tried to break through, seeing—nothing. So she dismissed the fear and grounded herself in imagination. Instead of worrying over the possibility of his return, she practiced twirling the silver baton, marshmallow-knobbed with white plastic at the ends, ignoring some flaking bits of silver on the metal. She wished for white boots with big red tassels, just like the majorettes at the high school wore when they pranced out ahead of the marching band, which formed and re-formed itself into shapes as it marched, reconfiguring itself into a drum, a star, into loops and interlacing circles before dissolving into another set of lines, marching to the stands, leaving the field empty and green and waiting for the game to proceed.

After the sunlight died, the relatives drifted out into the night, back to their own homes. The friends, though, remained while her mama fumed and sighed and sobbed over where Johnny Lee might be. Had that slutty ex-girlfriend picked him up at the foot of the dirt road, out of the family's line of vision? How had he managed to slip through the crowd? Ginny's mama blew her nose a lot and smoked cigarette after cigarette while others cursed Johnny Lee Fowler for a low-life piece of nothing that meant nothing but misery. "But I love him," her mama said, as if that answered all arguments.

Her mama had loved Ginny's real daddy, too, even though he was not a nice man, either. Ginny had vague memories of her oldest brother screaming with the sting of a leather belt, of her mother leaning over the sink while her busted nose bled a slick sheet of red to the porcelain, of a shotgun trained on them all. She remembered wishing her daddy away, wishing him dead. And it had worked, when her daddy was killed in an automobile accident on Highway 59, exactly one year before Johnny Lee moved in with them.

Late that night, Ginny sat on the floor beside Barbie's Dream House, the heavy cardboard case open to reveal upstairs and downstairs rooms full of colorful, modern, clean-lined furniture, though the cardboard was bent in at a table corner here, torn on a chair leg there. She imagined Barbie as a beautiful majorette in a satin uniform and marched the doll naked across the floor of the Dream House, Barbie's plastic feet perpetually arched for stilettos; black eyelashes forever swooped up solid; mounded breasts fixed, unmoving, and devoid of nipples. Barbie marched across the scatter of toys on the floor to the beat of a marching song, and up and over the arm of the empty chair, then up and across its back to the other arm. "It's time to go to sleep, Virginia Anne," her mama slurred and sighed, laying her head down on her arms as she sat at the kitchen table, while her best friend made a pot of coffee.

Ginny closed the Dream House—Barbie, Ken, Skipper, and all their furniture tucked away for the night—but as she turned to the hall, to go to bed among her brothers' calves and ankles, she noticed something very, very odd. It was something that certainly should have been noticed earlier, in all the uproar surrounding Johnny Lee's mysterious absence. Noticed by now had it been present before now, but it seemed simply to have dropped from thin air, from a hole torn in the ether, from a place of no logical explanation.

It was his cap—the purple and gold LSU cap—the one he wore always, turned to the side for TV and to the front for leaving. At this moment it was turned to the front, in the very middle of the seat of the La-Z-Boy recliner. Ginny walked over to the chair, eyes wide. She looked to those places in the rough fabric where a lit cigarette had left circles of melted black enmeshed in the material. There were burned marks on the TV table beside the chair as well, and a mound of butts in the honey-colored ashtray. The Old Charter bottle sat on the floor where he had left it, a strange sight, as the bottle always went wherever Johnny Lee went. Ginny nudged it with her big toe, sliding it closer to the chair, smiling, gazing at the empty chair, at the indentation of him, still pressed into the coarse, rumply upholstery.

She turned, but, one more time, out of the corner of her eye, came the pattern of plaid that was him, there in the dented foam where his body had born down, where the LSU cap now sat, facing front. She leaned close, and still closer to the cushioned seat where he had lounged, day in and day out, barking insults, picking at weaknesses, stick-poking at hidden angers, cementing insecurities. She looked into the weave of the fabric, deep into the threads loomed into one another, and a separate weave began to emerge. She squinted, adjusted, aligned her vision. There it was. There, within the pattern of burnt orange, the solid color of the chair, came another color, then another, as a new pattern emerged, though melded deep within the recliner's thick covering. It was the purple-and-gold plaid of his pajamas, forever imbedded in the depths of that chair, the place where, in selfish ignorance, he strode on the edge of a lost child's reconfiguration, the transcendence of her Santa Claus dreams. The presence of Johnny Lee Fowler had given Virginia a wish, and the ripening of that child's fresh wish had taken him into thin air, into the kind of forever such a child might one day believe in.

SUZANNE HUDSON's first novel, *In a Temple of Trees*, published in 2003, was a selection of the MystNoir Book Club. Her second novel, *In the Dark of the Moon*, was published in May 2005. A collection of short stories, *Opposable Thumbs*, which was a finalist for the John Gardner Fiction Award, was published in 2001. She lives in Fairhope, Alabama, where she is a middle-school guidance counselor and writing teacher.

Welcome to Monroe

Daniel Wallace

On the morning of the seventh day you knew they'd never find you. Not with dogs or with flashlights or with helicopters or handouts or all the men and women from town walking in lines through the woods so they wouldn't miss a thing. They would never find you because you couldn't be found. You were far away by then, somewhere near Monroe, Alabama. You knew that because that was the last sign you saw before he turned off that long stretch of main road. *Welcome To Monroe.* And the woods so deep and dark there, big enough to swallow the world. You were nothing inside of them. What a time for something like this to happen, days before Christmas, so close to Christmas that many of your presents were already wrapped and waiting beneath the tree. But this Christmas would be different from all the Christmases before it for your mother and your father and your brother and everyone who knew them, knew you. At school the teachers would take your friends aside and ask them questions, and then, when they began to cry, would let them talk to a man who knew what to say. The shadow of your absence would darken their world as your own world was darkened. But even so, you knew there would be other Christmases, and one day a long time away from this one all that had been fine and wonderful would be fine and wonderful again. Just not now and for some time to come.

Abernathy, your dog, had come the closest to finding you, and he was not even supposed to be looking. An old black-and-brown mutt who had wandered into your backyard three years ago, you pleaded with your parents to let you keep him, and they had agreed, if you promised to take care of him. And you did, in your bedroom. The dog ate there and slept there beside you. Abernathy (named after your favorite uncle) was your dog, completely. He followed you to school and waited there and walked back with you. He had been there when the man convinced you to get in his car, and watched as you drove away with him. He would not leave the corner where this happened, and when he was taken back home would return to that spot, day after day. He was still there, waiting, you were sure. The idea of it made you smile.

You could see things, even now, pictures of what was happening in your absence. It was amazing. You could see your house and your mother and father inside it and your brother in his room just lying on his bed looking at the ceiling and the pretty Christmas tree lights all dark and nothing now. But it wasn't clear really whether you were actually seeing it or were making up the pictures in your mind (or whatever your mind was now) from the crystal-clear memories you had of everybody and your life with them. You knew them so well, better than you had ever imagined. Your mother spent most of the day frozen, barely breathing. She looked like one of those wax figures in a museum. She only got up to cook dinner for her husband and son; somehow the fact that she was taking care of them made her at least partly alive, although she herself didn't eat. *Eat something*, your father said. *Just a bite.* But no. Your dad left the house before sunrise every morning to look for you, wearing his tan windbreaker and the Crimson Tide baseball cap. He didn't go to work or even think about going to work. Your brother tried not to change at all, going out with his friends, playing basketball, talking to girls. But there was a hollowness beneath his eyes, and everyone treated him kindly, too kindly, worried that any minute he might just break apart.

They would never find you. You knew what was happening to you, but they didn't, and this—the not-knowing—is what would haunt them. You knew that stories need an ending and that when they didn't have one people were unhappy. People like to read mysteries—you liked to read them—but they didn't like to have them in their lives, and that's what you were, would always be: a mystery. *The Mysterious Disappearance of Alyson McCrae.* Even a long time from now the mystery of your disappearance would occur to people you didn't even know, and they would wonder about it, and shake their heads. Without an ending there was always the possibility that what everyone thought happened hadn't, that you were somewhere in the world growing up, becoming a woman, living a life. As impossible as that was, there was always that possibility. That was your last and only wish: that they knew.

Never talk to strangers. That was the rule, and outside of the house it may have been the only rule, besides looking both ways before crossing the street, and you did both of them, without fail. But he wasn't a stranger. There were no strangers in your town; you knew almost everybody, more or less. You knew him less, but you knew him and he knew you, enough to call you by your full name: *Alyson Philadelphia McCrae.* Not everybody knew about the Philadelphia part. It was embarrassing, a ridiculous name you never understood. Your mom told you once it was where you were born, but you were born in Alabama, so that didn't make sense. "*Began* to be born, I said," she said. And then she smiled at you and rubbed your head. It was a pretty bad name though, and you never told anybody ("The P stands for *please mind your own business,"* you had been known to say), and so he must have heard it from your mom or dad. It was like saying a magic word—*abracadabra*—hearing him know this, assuming he knew your parents a lot better than he actually did. Though you pretended to be cautious for a minute or two after, you never thought there could be anything wrong with getting in his car.

"Everybody's okay," he said. "But your mom and dad had to run down to Dothan all of a sudden."

"Grandma?" you said.

He nodded. "She's been better," he said. "All signs point to a swift recovery, however. They just needed to get down there and make sure the doctors don't bury her by accident."

"She's a wildcat," you said. "She'd scrape her way out, they did that."

"You better believe it," he said. "Car's right here. Hop on in."

"What about Abernathy?"

The man froze up and you couldn't figure out why. Now you know, of course. He thought there was somebody else there, somebody he didn't know about. "Who's Abernathy?" he asked.

"My dog," you said.

"Oh. Abernathy. I can't have a dog in the car," he said. "I'm allergic. Can Abernathy make his way back home on his own?"

"He's the smartest dog in Alabama," you said. And you held his small pointy head in your hands and kissed him right between the eyes. "You go on home now Abernathy," you said. "Let's see who gets there first."

But Abernathy wouldn't move. He watched you get into the car and drive away, and when you turned around to look he was still there watching, getting smaller and smaller as you got farther and farther away.

How could no one have seen this? And again not for you, because even if they had it would have been way too late for you, but for your parents, for your brother, so they could have a place to set down their grief. In a town so small you knew everybody and everybody knew you. Maybe when it's like this, sometimes you're just taken for granted, invisible. Alyson McCrae wasn't news yet. She was just a little girl.

"This ain't the way home," you said. Now that you were in the car he figured he didn't have to pretend to be someone he wasn't, doing something he wasn't. He didn't have to pretend to be driving you home now.

"Maybe I know something you don't," he said.

"Like what?"

"Like maybe it's a shortcut."

"A longcut more like," you said. "You about can't get there from here."

"You sure have a mouth on you, Alyson Philadelphia McCrae," he said.

"Well this ain't the way," you said.

"I think you'll see," he said, smiling over at you and driving, tapping the steering wheel with his index finger with a steady beat, as though he heard a song only he could hear.

You would see, but by then it was way too late.

You kept trying to remember if you'd ever met him before as he drove out of town, past every farm you'd ever seen and then past those you hadn't. Maybe at a party your parents gave one time. That was it. "Alyson McCrae," he said. "It's a pleasure to meet you." You remembered now because he was an odd one. He was very skinny. He had a long face and right on top of it a forehead as big as Canada. His hair was thin too. You figure he had about eighteen hairs, all slicked back like they were worth the trouble. He had a small metal American flag pinned to the lapel of his jacket, which was brown. You thought you'd never seen him before but he knew your middle name so you figured there was something, some relationship, a bond between this man and your family, otherwise there is no way in the world you would have gotten into his car. No way in the world. But there was nothing you could do now.

"I don't know you," you said.

He was quiet now, driving, still drumming his finger against the steering wheel.

"I want you to take me home," you said.

But it was as if you weren't even there.

ON THE MORNING OF the seventh day you knew they'd never find you. But the truth is you really didn't know what day it was: it might have been the seven hundredth day, or the seven thousandth. Maybe everybody was dead, everybody you knew and everybody who knew you. Everybody was dead, and everybody died the same way, with the mystery inside of them, the mystery of what had happened to Alyson Philadelphia McCrae.

Why? How long had you spent wondering why? What did you do that was so bad? How had you lived in the world that you would deserve to die like this? You reviewed every moment you could remember—and there were a lot of moments, twelve years of them—and you came up with nothing. There was no reason. Things happened. Bad things, good things. Like Abernathy just wandering into the yard one day and becoming your warm and steady pal. And Janice, Maria, and Kristy, your three really good friends you never even met before this year. And the mother you had, and the father, and the brother—people who never let a whole day go by without letting you know in some way how much they loved you. What had you done to deserve all this sweetness?

Nothing. Things like this just happened. Nearly Christmas now it seemed, and then that car, that man, that day. There was no real difference between the whys of the love and hate. Except the love was better.

Writer and illustrator DANIEL WALLACE was born and raised in Birmingham, Alabama. His writings include *Ray in Reverse*, *The Watermelon King*, and his first novel, *Big Fish*, which was adapted for the screen in 2003 by Tim Burton and John August. His illustrations have been reproduced for variety of products including T-shirts and greeting cards and have been featured in the *L.A. Times* and *Italian Vanity Fair*. He currently resides in Chapel Hill with his wife, Laura, and son, Henry.

ACKNOWLEDGMENTS

Jim Gilbert & Gail Waller

In putting this entertaining little volume together, we were not alone. Grateful thanks to:

Carolyn Newman, our publisher—this anthology is her brainchild and, so we hope, her delight.

Ashley Gordon laid the groundwork by assembling an initial list of contributors, assisted greatly by Carolyn Haines and the inimitable Barbara Peters.

Amy Halpin helped us bulldog this book through the early editing stages.

Our in-house production manager, Lissa Monroe, effortlessly came up with the perfect title only after we trudged through a veritable swamp of unusable B-movie slogans.

And of course, for their time and their sweat, huge thanks to all of the authors featured in these pages—including Julia Spencer-Fleming for her introduction and Daniel Wallace for his terrific illustrations.